I0620263

HOUSE OF CONSEQUENCE
Book One of the DeGaul Family Series

Copyright 2014 Nienna Luinwe
Published by Pink Cat Press at Smashwords

Acknowledgements

To my sister Beverly,

Thank you for all your support and research. I really couldn't have done it without you. I am fully aware that without you, it would have taken me much longer to achieve my goal. Thank you for your support.

To Robert,

Thank you for being my original muse. Your input helped me shape my story. Thank you for all your support and technical details. Thank you for being such a wonderful muse and friend.

To Steven,

Thank you for all the hours you spent editing and rewriting my creation. Thank you for being my support and inspiration and for all the encouragement you gave unconditionally. Your love and support carries me daily.

Prologue
Paris, France September 1987

It was early on a beautiful crisp Friday morning. People were milling about on the walkways and streets of Paris beginning their busy lives while he sat at a tiny table in front of Le Patisserie Laurent Duchene waiting for his partner to arrive. He sat watching them go about their business while sipping his steamy cup of coffee. Casually, he forked small pieces of his Napoléon/Mille-Feuille, a delicate pastry whose literal translation means a thousand sheets and is made with many layers of puff pastry with cream in between each layer, into his mouth while he methodically studied the comings and goings of every person within his line of sight.

While he waited for his partner to reveal himself, he contemplated his decision. He knew his Malcolm would be very unhappy about his decision. Unhappy being an extremely grievous understatement, however, but it had to be done. He understood that the life he'd chosen was much too dangerous for him to just walk away from and start a family, but much to his surprise, he'd found himself longing for just that, a family. She had bombarded her way into his life and was all he could think about. She was a complete and total distraction and, in his line of work, distractions could get you killed. So, he had had to choose between the two of

3

them. His career, or make this unique opportunity for a different, more settled lifestyle, come to fruition. The decision had almost been too easy. He'd been an operative for over fifteen years and he'd realized that he was ready for a change. In fact, he needed this lifetime change of venue. Operatives had a shelf-live, an expiration date and he preferred not to find out when his was due to expire. So, he'd decided to close the book on this chapter of his life and begin a new one. He would later find out that it just wasn't that easy to achieve.

He spotted Malcolm walking wearily through the bustling street toward him. He was exposed and out in the open, but he wasn't worried. There was no operation going on at the moment and this was their down time. Besides, he'd already staked the place out and knew it was safe for them to meet there and he was sure that Malcolm had done the same or he would have warned him off otherwise. To be safe, they never sat together at the same table just in case an enemy was nearby or was somehow tracking one of them. Their specialized ear pieces activated the moment they were in range of each other and they began speaking in low inaudible tones that no one around them could hear. To anyone observing them, it would appear as though both men were separately enjoying their reading materials while eating their breakfast and drinking their coffee completely unaware of one another.

"Malcolm."

"Vincent." They greeted one another discreetly, without turning, while they both casually pretended to read the current day's newspaper. They sat with their backs facing one another at two different tiny tables on the boulevard, each seemingly absorbed in the material in front of him. The waiter made his way to Malcolm's table and took his order for a cup of coffee. When the waiter returned with Malcolm's coffee and had made his way back to the table where Vincent sat, refilled his cup and gone away again, they began speaking to one another again.

"Why am I here Vince? I thought we were off for a while?" Malcolm asked in a hushed irritated tone. His lips were barely moving.

"I wanted you to know that...," he hesitated, "...that I would not be returning to Ops."

"What? Why?" The shock and annoyance contained in Malcolm's voice was barely masked. "What the hell is going on?" "This is no time for jokes and games Vince. We have no time for frivolity!"

"I'm not joking Mal. I've decided to change my lifestyle. I'm getting out while I'm still young and more importantly, alive!"

"It's because of *her* isn't it?" He said incredulously. Malcolm couldn't believe what he was hearing. "I told you not to become involved with her! I told you not to become involved with that woman!"

"It isn't your decision Mal. Nor is it your life. I..."

Malcolm cut him off. "Damn you for this!" Displaying no emotion that anyone watching would notice, yet seething with anger, he casually folded his newspaper and paid his bill. Finishing his coffee and preparing to leave he said, "This isn't the end Vince. Not by a long shot! You can't break up a long standing partnership on a whim and especially not because of a woman. I won't stand for it. I won't let you end things because of her. "This…" he said through clinched teeth, "…is NOT the end! It can't be Vince. You know as well as I do that this life never lets us go."

"It is for me old friend. I'm letting it go. I can't live this life any longer. I want normalcy Mal. Surely you can understand that."

Malcolm sighed. His initial shock and anger subsiding. "I can. I long for it too. However, you know me. I'm in this for life. I can't settle down. I'm married to this life for life. I wish you the best of luck my friend. Just…" Malcolm hesitated. "…watch your back. We've made plenty of enemies. If any of them find out who you really are, you could lose everything and everyone close to you, especially after this last assignment. If you're planning to disappear with this particular woman, you damn well better cover your ass and leave all traces of Vincent St. Claire and her behind.

The line between them, via their ear pieces, went dead as Malcolm disappeared around a busy corner.

Vince calmly finished his coffee and breakfast fifteen minutes later. He paid his bill and casually strolled down the boulevard in the opposite direction towards his new future.

Chapter One - Present Day

Home at last… Geneviève thought, taking in the view from the kitchen of her ten thousand square foot mansion by the clear blue-green ocean. The flight from her offices in Los Angeles had been long. And, even though she made the flight several times a year, she was always impatient to return home to her very own private paradise. Geneviève made trips all over the world. She was one of many creative individuals in her family. A gift she'd inherited from her mother who was a world renowned artist herself.

While her mother created works of art with paints and clay, Geneviève, (pronounced "ZHAWN-vee-EHV"), had taken an interest in gemstones and fabrics. Her mother, Alexis DeGaul, owned many prestigious art galleries all over the world. The most popular and largest galleries were located in Milan, Paris and Rome. She also owns galleries in New York, Los Angeles and San Francisco. Unlike her brothers who followed in the footsteps of their father, Andre DeGaul, in his international businesses, Geneviève chose the path her mother had chosen and opted to hone her creative skills. She managed the family's galleries that were stateside and her mother the ones overseas.

The house was a gift from her father. The expansive ten bedroom, fourteen bathroom, home was indeed grand. The layout was open and airy with high vaulted ceilings and lots and lots and lots of windows. Every room in the house had a spectacular view. The front of the house was perfectly manicured with lush island greenery and an absolutely stunning view of Mount Walaleale in the not too far distance. The Wallua River State Park butted up against her property lines and most of her neighbors, including herself, were avid hikers, bikers, and horseback riders. They all had their own horses which were boarded on the outer edge of the tiny community. Electric golf carts were used regularly to get around within their private community. The rear and sides of the house were almost entirely glass. Her view was of the majestic Pacific Ocean and her private beach. She loved waking to the sound of the waves crashing onto the beach. The tranquility of the ocean sounds relaxed her and she slept deeply and soundly every night in her huge eastern king four-poster bed covered by a very pale pink, sheer and shimmery fabric. The soft lovely fabric was a nod to her girly side which she treasured and nurtured.

She lived there year-round with her constant companion Sergeant, and enjoyed her expansive private beach whenever she could manage the time to do so. It was part of a very secluded and very exclusive neighborhood on the eastern side of the warm tropical island of Kauai's Coconut Coast. There were only a few homes on this part of the island and she knew all of her neighbors.

She smiled to herself knowing that even though it was early in the morning, the temperature outside was warm and inviting. She began her morning ritual, only this time without the added stress of her family, her brother Pierre to be precise. As CEO of the family's Security and Operations division, he was responsible for everyone's safety and could be quite the tyrant when he wanted to be and she adored him. Pierre, accompanied by her security detail, would arrive tomorrow afternoon. But for now, Geneviève was alone. It was just she and Sergeant.

Sergeant, her two year old male German shepherd, was a gift from Pierre. He'd decided he was tired of trying to keep up with her due to her uncanny ability to shake her security detail for privacy. He just showed up on her birthday with this little black and tan eight week old ball of fur and announced, "Félicitations! You are now the proud owner of the most fearsome creature on the planet!" He held the puppy in front of her for inspection.

Geneviève looked at the pup skeptically and replied sarcastically. "Really?"

Pierre retorted, "Absolutely! Just give him a little time and lots of training. You'll see." He winked at her and she smiled and laughed at him.

"I'm tired of trying to keep up with you Evie. You're constantly ditching your security detail. Please take him." Pierre pleaded. "I promise you won't regret it. Once he's fully trained, I promise to call off the two-legged dogs I have following you around now. You will have your beloved privacy. But, you'll have to promise to keep this killer with you at all times." He said smiling.

Geneviève sighed and gazed into the squirming puppy's big liquid brown eyes. For a long moment, they simply stared at one another, then, she finally spoke.

"What do you call him?" she inquired. Not taking her eyes off the pup.

"That's up to you Evie." Pierre replied while systematically mentally crossing his fingers and toes.

"How big will he get Pierre?" She asked, finally breaking the spell between them and looking into her big brother's earnest hopeful eyes.

"Oh, he'll get about eighty-five to one hundred pounds, maybe a little more. Pierre began talking fast. "He's got champion blood lines Evie! His parents are both blue ribbon champions in agility and…"

Geneviève threw up a hand in his face to shut him up. "Stop! I don't care about his bloodlines Pierre. I'm not that uptight! I do care about the mess he may make around my house and…"

She stopped talking when she saw the pleading look in her brother's dark brown eyes. Without saying another word, she took the whining, squirming pup from him and held him at eye level.

"You're a bit puny for a bodyguard" she said. "But, I suppose I'd rather have you following me around than some big burly, bossy, hairy, knuckle dragging gang of men!"

Pierre hadn't realized that he'd been holding his breath the entire time she was making her decision. "Merci." He said softly. "Like I said, you won't regret it."

That was two years ago, and Pierre had been right, she hadn't regretted her decision. Now she and Serge were fully trained. Pierre had insisted that she be the one to handle him during his training to insure their bond. As Serge's primary handler, she would also be able to customize her commands for him. The training had been challenging at times but Serge turned out to be very smart and learned quickly. She trained him on verbal commands in French, German and English accompanied by hand signals and whistles. Best of all, they had developed a mutual admiration for one another and were practically inseparable. She truly couldn't imagine life without him. She looked down at him and smiled.

She ate her light breakfast of toast and fresh fruit, strawberries and bananas, her favorite, and a hot cup of mint green tea. Serge was also enjoying his breakfast at his own designer pet eatery station. His bowls were mounted in the kitchen wall and elevated perfectly to his height. The water bowl held up to six cups of water and was hooked up to a waterline that provided him with fresh water twenty-four hours a day. It even had its own on/off switch. Throughout her home and her property she accommodated him by installing freshwater doggy drinking fountains so he wouldn't have to go all the way to the kitchen for a drink of water. She marveled at how attached she had become to her furry companion. He had almost as many accessories as she did. He even had his own bathroom, modified to fit his doggy needs. It included his very own doggy shower and spa tub, bone shaped of course. She laughed softly to herself.

Her kitchen was fully stocked. Bernard, her uncle acted as her butler, and his wife Lucy, her maid and her mother's baby sister, were notified ahead of time that she would be arriving within the week. Bernard greeted her with a smile and a kiss on her forehead. "Bonjour Missy." He said cheerfully as he entered the kitchen. "Enjoying your breakfast? Did your meetings go well on the mainland?"

"Oui, I am and yes they did. Thank you for asking" she answered with a smile of her own. "Oncle?" she said questioningly. "You've been calling me Missy my entire life!" She said laughing. "Will you ever call me by my given name?"

"Heavens no, Missy! Why would I do that?" He replied, feigning surprise by the question. "Besides, I have not been calling you Missy all your life. I have been calling you Little Miss Missy due to your very precocious personality and independent nature. I have simply shortened it throughout the years to just Missy." They laughed simultaneously.

"Okay, okay, I give up!" she said, still laughing.

"Serge has his annual veterinary appointment this morning Missy." He reminded her.

"That's right! I totally forgot." She said.

"I'll take him for you" Bernard volunteered. "You enjoy your breakfast and workout. We'll be back before you know it."

"All right, sure, that would be great!" Geneviève said. "Merci, Oncle!"

"No problem Missy. Besides, your brute and I need some alone time anyway." He said chuckling. "Don't we boy?" Bernard reached down to scratch Serge's ears. Brutus was Bernard's nickname for Sergeant. They, too, had a mutual admiration thing going. Serge loved Bernard and his wife Lucy and they loved him.

"Lucy should be along shortly Missy. She stopped by the market to pick up a few things for dinner this evening." He said over his shoulder as he and Serge headed for the garage door.

"Merci Oncle B!" she said.

Oncle B and Tante Luce have been the names she called them for as long as she could remember. Lucy had been her Au-pair. She'd helped her mother take care of Geneviève throughout her infancy and childhood. Bernard and Lucy came with the house. When her parents decided to move back to the mainland, Bernard and Lucy opted to stay here on the island with Geneviève. Her parents agreed so they stayed. Bernard was formally her parent's butler and Lucy was their maid. Both were in their late twenties when they began working for her parents as the story went. It was a fairytale story. They fell in love with the family they worked for and eventually each other. Now, they worked for her. If you wanted to call it work. It had an uncanny resemblance to one big, stable, happy family. They had two children of their own, a boy and a girl. Josephine was born first and three years younger than Geneviève. They became fast friends and were more like sisters than friends. Their second child, a son, Rogét, pronounced ("Row-jay"), was an Architect now and ran the Electronics division of her father's vast business empire. He was best friends with her middle brother Míchel. Bernard and Lucy lived on the premises in one of the cottage homes on her property.

She sat reminiscing about her childhood, over breakfast, in the stillness of her kitchen and watched the ocean crash its surf onto the beach and the sea birds hunt up their morning meals.

After breakfast, Geneviève worked out in her fully equipped onsite gym, and then took a long hot shower. She washed her hair first and then her body. Not bothering to dry her hair in the process of drying her body because she was going to have to wash it lightly again once she finished her morning dip in the ocean.

She loved the warmth of the sea water though she never ventured out too far. She had no desire to become some hungry confused shark's meal. The house boasted an indoor/outdoor swimming pool that she used when she wanted to actually swim.

Geneviève put on her two-piece bathing suit, the white one that resembled a baby doll. It had thin straps that tied behind her long graceful neck, a bra top with a sheer chiffon-like fabric that enveloped her tiny waist leaving her abs exposed. The suit's bottom was a thong. She loved thongs. They showed off her derrière in the most flattering way. Around her waist, she tied the matching sarong which was made out of the same sheer, silky, chiffon-like fabric. She wasn't worried about offending anyone because there were only two houses in her area and no one from the resorts ever venture down quite this far due to the very efficient on-site community security personnel. The security was set up and managed by her brother Pierre, of course. Her father developed the tiny community after all. It wasn't a gated community. Her father was adamant about keeping it open so it didn't have the feeling of a compound. But it was regularly patrolled by well trained security personnel most of whom had previous military experience in special operations and the like. Everyone who owned a home in the exclusive and secluded community felt very safe there. So, she knew she'd be alone in her very own private paradise. Or at least that's what she thought…

She picked up her towel and blanket and headed for the door. She would spend her morning wading in the warm welcoming waters of her little part of the very big ocean outside her beautiful piece of paradise and lounge on her private beach soaking up the morning sun's warm rays.

Chapter Two

Right on time, Bryce thought to himself, as he looked out his windows towards the beach. Pierre's little sister, Evie, was right on her very predictable schedule. Bryce purchased the house next door years ago so he could be close to the family, now he stayed there mostly to watch over Evie. She was fully aware that he was there and she politely ignored him most of the time. She was nice and neighborly enough but kept to herself for the most part. He didn't intrude on her privacy which was the key to surveying her. He wasn't sure if she knew about the arrangement that he and Pierre had agreed upon. Probably not, since she remained polite when they, accidently on purpose, ran into each other as neighbors or in the town's grocery store.

Her parents, Andre and Alexis DeGaul became his guardians when his own parents were killed in a car accident when he was sixteen. Both families had been very close and it was a tragedy to all left behind. Bryce was an only child and orphaned. Andre and Alexis DeGaul were his legal guardians according to his parent's Living Trust and they stepped in and made him an official DeGaul. Andre insisted that he keep the last name that he was born with in order to maintain his lineage, but also gave him the option to hyphenate using the DeGaul name as well. Bryce was very happy his parents had prearranged for the DeGaul's to be his legal guardians in the event that something happened to them. The DeGaul's nurtured and loved him and made him a permanent part of their family unit. They put him through college and made him a partner in the DeGaul business empire. He was the Executive Vice President of the Security Division, second in command under Pierre.

Andre DeGaul was an international businessman, recently semi-retired, who had his fingers in pies all over the globe and he was very protective when it came to his baby girl. All of the men in her family were including himself he mused. But Bryce did not see Geneviève as Pierre's little sister anymore. She was a beautiful, almost mythical creature and he wanted her for himself and that was a potential problem.

The youngest of three siblings, Geneviève Papillion DeGaul was the moon and the stars to her brothers and her father. She was ten years younger than Pierre and seven years under Míchel. They protected and loved her fiercely. It was definitely a dilemma indeed. And then, there was her fur covered razor blade, Sergeant. Bryce had had a hand in training him. He thanked the universe for that. Serge wouldn't let anyone near her, especially men he was unfamiliar with. Oh, she could make him back down if she wanted to, but, to Bryce, it seemed she liked the idea of keeping men at bay. Bryce, however, was the exception. Serge visited him regularly when they were on the beach. He'd trot right over for some scratches and resume his post by her side. He even seemed to love the ocean as much as she did.

Momentarily lost in his thoughts of the past, his memory drifted back to when Andre and Alexis brought Geneviève home from the hospital. He and his parents visited them a few days later to welcome their new addition. It was strange to him because he remembered not knowing that the DeGaul's had been expecting a child. Being the tender age of six years old himself when she was born, he reasoned that he was probably more interested in his toys and playing outside, than someone being pregnant. Still, he wondered sometimes.

At that time, Geneviève had been the smallest person he had ever seen. He was amazed and enthralled with the tiny ethereal creature that was placed in his arms that day. Because he was six years old and almost a man in his eyes, he felt he could handle such a big responsibility as long as he was sitting down. Pictures were taken that day of all the children together and then both families. His mother, Grace Marten, and Alexis were lifelong best friends, so taking pictures of both families together for this momentous event was a must. Thinking back, he remembered her looking up at him with those startling grey-green eyes. Even then, they were mesmerizing.

There had been many changes in the DeGaul household that first year of Evie's life. Bernard St. Claire began working for them a few weeks after she was born. And, shortly after Bernard arrived, Lucy, Alexis's baby sister, came to stay with her and help out with the newborn. Bernard and Lucy traveled everywhere with the family.

He remembered Evie as an inquisitive little girl who followed him and her brothers everywhere when they were teenagers. The families would get together when time and opportunities allowed, which wasn't often. When she grew into an awkward teenager, she still followed Bryce and her brothers absolutely everywhere. She was proud and defiant, strong-willed and very independent. Qualities Bryce loved in the female form. Geneviève hadn't changed much over the years with one very noticeable exception, she was *all* woman now. Sexy as sin and Bryce wanted her bad.

Because their families were internationally connected, there would often be quite some time between visits. Bryce saw Evie only a few times as a baby. Then, again, when she was a small child of four or five and he was almost a teen. The next time he saw her was at his own parent's funeral. It was a sad tragic day and everyone seemed to be in a sort of emotional limbo. The DeGaul's had been and still were very good to him. When Bryce turned eighteen he moved out of the main house and into one of the small two bedroom cottages on the property given to him by the DeGaul's. Andre sent him to college and gave him a job in the Security division of his company working with Pierre.

Embracing his memories, Bryce watched Evie make her way down to her private beach where she swam almost every morning in the warm salty water. He shook his head to clear the images of her as a child and teen and resumed watching her and her surroundings. He wondered how much she knew about her father and his business dealings. His guess was that she knew nothing. Andre DeGaul was very powerful. His image as a deadly, dangerous man of extreme business integrity and moral content seemed to have validity. Bryce was witness to the way he carried out his business decisions. At times, brutal, but always fair. Andre DeGaul didn't believe in backdoor business deals or anything illegal. He kept his deals fair and honest where everyone would benefit. Even if it was a hostile takeover, he made sure that almost none of the employees lost their jobs.

Despite all Andre DeGaul's efforts to be fair and impartial, someone was on a mission to destroy him and the family name. Even more disturbing were the threats that had begun to surface. The family's security had been tightened as a precaution, and that's how Bryce came to be standing in silent and secret watch over Geneviève.

Andre DeGaul was a loving family man. He cared deeply about his family and protected them fiercely. A few years ago, the family began to receive threats. No one knew who the culprit was. Not even Andre and it was now Bryce and Pierre's job to find out. Threats to the family had been made and needed to be addressed. That was the real reason Pierre had insisted Geneviève take that pup two years ago. He was worried. They all were. Everyone felt that Geneviève was the most precious addition to their family and, because of her disappearing acts, the most vulnerable. Her brothers and father would all be destroyed if anything ever happened to her.

Geneviève had been their miracle baby. During the end of her pregnancy, her mother was in a car accident. Her vehicle was rear ended and the force of the collision sent her into labor prematurely. The baby was in severe distress and an emergency cesarean had to be performed because her mother's placenta had become separated from her uterus and the baby was suffocating. Her mother was also bleeding internally. Doctors worked quickly and diligently to save them both. Obviously, they had been successful because Evie was alive and well today and Alexis didn't look any worse for the wear. Although, Bryce sometimes struggled trying to remember that day when they came home from the hospital with Evie, he didn't remember Alexis being injured at all. In fact, she seemed, in a word, normal. Pushing those unproductive thoughts aside, it was he and Pierre's job to keep everyone safe. So, for now, they were devising a plan to do just that.

It started with Sergeant for Evie. Since Pierre was in charge of the family's security division and Bryce was his right hand, they were bound and determined to keep everyone safe until the threat was neutralized. Each female family member was assigned a canine companion. Even Alexis had one, a big male German shepherd named Beau who was her shadow and traveled all over the world with her. Being the only two DeGaul women, they were never to leave home without their canine companions. And, for the most part, they didn't.

Babysitting Geneviève, however, was turning out to be a tricky and very sticky situation that that damned Pierre had talked him into, again. Bryce thought to himself. But, Pierre was the brother that Bryce never had and he would do just about anything for him. They had, over the years, saved each other lives time and time again. Their friendship was solidified in blood, literally as well as in name. Since Bryce had purchased the home next to the DeGaul estate there on the island in order to remain close to his adopted family years ago, it was simple to keep Evie under surveillance when she was home. He was at home, and, at the same time, he could keep his promise to Pierre that he would keep an eye on his little sister and keep her safe.

He continued to watch her as she organized her things, spreading out her blanket and towel on the sand preparing to go for her morning swim. Geneviève never ventured very far into the water. She would go out until the water was just at her hips then she would simply float on the waves with her face turned into the sun.

There was something different this morning though. He knew when she was in town because Bernard and Lucy always showed up a day or two before to prepare for her arrival. They typically stayed in their own place on the property, but milled about the house doing what they do before she came home. He also knew when she was due back home because he trailed her every movement everywhere she went. But, where was everybody? The realization hit him like a ton of bricks. He stood stock still as his eyes moved from her to her surroundings to inside her house, then back to her. My God, is it possible that she's alone? He thought. Regaining his composure, he looked for signs of life in her house again. Nothing, no brothers, no bodyguards, not even the damn dog was anywhere to be seen. His curiosity and growing concern were beginning to become overwhelming as was his desire for this woman he considered his forbidden fruit.

Geneviève was never, truly, left alone. Pierre had Bryce secretly following her all over the world because his little sister was known to, and expected to, attempt to give her security detail the slip. So far, she had been so very frustratingly successful in the past, but Bryce had never lost her. She may have been able to give those men the slip, but not Bryce. She, of course, was completely unaware of his following her and he wanted to keep it that way. The only time he ever revealed his presence was here on this island. And, at the moment, he felt it was time he did just that.

Bryce began to think fast. What the hell was she doing here alone? Did Pierre know she was here? Where was that damned fur covered razor blade dog? Deciding to investigate, he grabbed a beach blanket and headed for the door. He decided to leave his khaki colored cargo pants and matching t-shirt on. He needed a reason to open dialog between them and this was a perfect opportunity.

He began muttering to himself… "Where is everybody? Where's my furry friend, Evie? Oh, good morning by the way…" He was babbling and tongued tied and he knew it. Because, if she figured out that her brother put him up to being her invisible bodyguard, she'd kill them both he mused. But before he made it out his door he noticed movement in her house. Bryce froze where he stood, straining to make out the two figures moving strategically through the DeGaul beach house. He realized very quickly that these men were not there for a friendly social call. Dressed in all black from head to toe, they were systematically searching each room. Then, he spotted two other men making their way down to the beach where Geneviève was sitting with her back to them. Bryce raced back to his bedroom for his .9mm that he kept in the nightstand next to his bed. Slipped it behind his back loaded and ready, picked up several extra magazines and made a dash for the door.

Chapter Three

Four men, arriving in a sleek black BMW 750Li xDrive Sedan, parked in Geneviève's driveway. When they got out of the vehicle two of the men headed around opposite sides of the house and towards the rear beach side of the house and the other two began to casually make their way to the front door. They rang the bell several times and no one answered.

Let's let the boss know that no one answered." One man said to the other. They quickly made their way off the expansive porch and walked to the side of the house where they found him.

He stood, watching her, understanding immediately why his employer was so very intrigued. She was an exquisite beauty.

He had already deduced that she was alone and was reveling in his luck when two of his men appeared beside him.

"Boss, no one is home."

"Yes, I know." He growled. He was a tall man of six foot six inches, long dark shoulder-length hair that he'd tied back with a leather cord, and calculatingly cold black eyes. He was watching Geneviève on the beach applying suntan oil to her body. He turned to them and stated in a calm yet commanding voice.

"She's on the beach. If no one is with her, this will be that much easier. Now, we need to get down there, get her and get out of here before someone does show up! Erik, you come with me. Tito, you and Vance search the interior. This shouldn't take long. "And Tito," He stated with malice. "Don't waste time on any rooms she doesn't use. Leave her bedroom to me. Once we have collected her, I will search it myself." Good help was so difficult to attain these days. He thought to himself.

"Yes sir!" Tito replied as he made his way to the rear entrance of the beach house.

"Vance…"

"Sir…"

"Make sure his retarded ass doesn't fuck up. If he does, terminate his employment…permanently."

"Yes sir." Vance nodded and turned to follow Tito into the house.

Turning to Erik he said, "Let's get the girl and get her to the car." Erik nodded and they began their descent down to the beach.

Chapter Four

Geneviève finished her swim and headed back to her blanket. Completely relaxed now, she began her routine of applying a protective layer of tanning oil to her already honey colored skin. She picked up the bottle and poured some of the sweet vanilla scented liquid into her soft delicate hands. As she began applying the oil to her shapely legs, she knew he was watching her again. He, being her older brother Pierre's very handsome childhood friend and her neighbor, Bryce Marten, had been watching her since the moment she stepped out onto their little private beach. Geneviève knew this because she'd spotted him in the window before she stepped out of her own house. One of the advantages of having bay windows, she thought to herself. She had had her suspicions as to why he seemed to always be at home when she was but she had no proof that anything was out of the ordinary. Added to that, he never bothered her or interrupted her privacy. He kept his distance behaving more like a sleek black panther stalking his prey than a neighbor, she mused. She supposed it could have been worse. Pierre could have contrived a full protective detail and she would have big burly men all over her home and her privacy and peace would cease to exist altogether. That, she thought, would have been intolerable. So, having Bryce right next door didn't bother her. In fact, it was a comfort of sorts, she thought smiling to herself, though she would never ever admit that to him or her brother. She would just continue to allow them to believe they were doing their surveillance incognito. She laughed to herself.

Without alerting him that she knew he was watching her, she smoothed more oil onto her other leg taking care to pay special attention to her feet. She had nice feet she'd been told. Small and delicate like her hands. She had soft flawless caramel colored skin that was warm to the touch. She inherited her skin, shapely legs, curvy hips, a tight round butt, a tiny waist and a full natural bosom that many women paid obscene amounts of money to attain from her mother whose heritage was a mix of French Creole, Black and Native American Choctaw. Her long honey brown hair which was shiny, luxuriously thick, and curly cascaded around her face. She had her mother's startling grey eyes with hints of green made even more interesting with their flecks of gold. The almond shape of her eyes, her high cheek bones along with her full lips, she'd inherited from her father who was Native American Cherokee and Black. She was a striking, exotic beauty, although she did not see herself that way. To her, she was just Geneviève. She was Pierre and Míchel's little sister and daddy's little girl. She smiled at the thought of the overbearing men in her life. They doted on her.

Spoiled her rotten and protected her from everyone and everything. She hated it! She could and would take care of herself. Okay, maybe she didn't hate the spoiling so much. That part she loved if she was going to be honest with herself. She had always been stubborn and independent though. Traits that she knew drove her brothers crazy. She laughed out loud again.

Lost in the revelry of her thoughts, she did not hear the footsteps approaching in the warm sand. A shadow fell over her and she stiffened. She thought she knew who it was because there was only one other person near her, right? Then, a second shadow fell over her and Geneviève knew something was terribly wrong.

Before she could turn to see who had encroached on her private time and property, she was lifted out of her seated position and restrained. Her assailant covered her mouth with a damp, sickly smelling cloth and she struggled to free herself from his grasp. The other man stepped in front of her and smiled menacingly. He had a terrible scar across his left cheek from his temple to his top lip. He was tall, broad shouldered in a brawny sort of way with a Mediterranean complexion. His hair was shoulder length, oily and combed straight back held in place at the nape of his neck with what looked like a leather cord. His voice was just as oily as his hair when he spoke to her.

"Mademoiselle DeGaul, do not struggle. I am Horus Drakkar. I will be your host and keeper for awhile." he said confidently. His voice had the whisper of an exotic yet, somewhat French, accent.

Geneviève, now completely panicked, began to slip into darkness. The last thing she saw was the inauspicious smile of the scarred man.

"Put her in the car." He ordered. Erik lifted Geneviève's limp body and they began trekking through the sand back to their car in her driveway.

Chapter Five

Bryce knew he didn't have much time. He also knew that there was no cover on the beach so confronting Geneviève's attackers on the beach was not an option. Moving quickly and quietly to the front of his estate, he quickly assessed the distance between the two houses and the time it would take the two men to return to their vehicle carrying Geneviève's listless body. He sprinted the distance using the multitude of Kukui trees, Banyan trees and gardenia bushes for cover. Once he was on the DeGaul grounds he silently and deliberately made his way to the front where he knew the men must have parked their vehicle. He took up a crouched hidden position behind two blooming Royal Poinciana trees. It made a perfect ambush location. The trees were almost thirty feet tall. Their graceful twisted limbs and flat lush, green, fern-like canopy in full bloom with massive clusters of bright, flame-red flowers, casted and displaced shadows. Between them were pink and purple bougainvillea vines that he used to his advantage.

There were two cars parked in her horseshoe shaped driveway, a chocolate metallic 2012 Bugatti Veyron convertible, Geneviève's car, and a black BMW 750Li with no one in sight. He knew that the gunmen were armed with automatic weapons so Bryce calculated that he would have to take them out one at a time stealthily and very, *very*, quickly.

Just as he was formulating his plan, two men appeared, one with Geneviève's slack body still in his arms and the other man he recognized immediately. Shock, disbelief and then fury hit him all at once. Horus Drakkar? What the hell was he doing here? What did he want with Geneviève? More importantly, who was he working for?

He was a thug, a ruthless, maniacal private contractor for hire to anyone willing to pay for his so-called services. The man had absolutely no scruples or moral values and had a reputation of unrestrained ruthlessness. He was a well-known hired gun used by many to do their dirty work and he would do anything as long as the money was worth his time. Just then, the men that had been inside Geneviève's house stepped out onto the porch. Bryce waited and listened.

"Put her in the car and stay here. I need to search her quarters personally." He barked out his orders. "You two come with me." Drakkar signaled for Erik and Vance to follow him back into Geneviève's house.

Bryce hesitated. Now, with only one bad guy, his odds of success were much better. He wouldn't even have to break a sweat he thought to himself. As Drakkar and his two henchmen disappeared into the house, Bryce made his move. The man left behind to guard Geneviève was too busy settling her in the back seat of the BMW to notice Bryce approaching. As he stood to close her door, Bryce hit him over the head with the butt of his gun and the man dropped to the ground like a stone. Bryce quickly unlatched Geneviève's seatbelt and lifted her out of the seat. He noticed her purse on the floor of the back seat and grabbed that too, hoping her car keys were in it. How thoughtful of them to remember her purse he thought to himself sarcastically. Bryce placed Evie in the passenger's seat of her car, secured her seatbelt and ran back to the man lying on the ground. He searched the man and took his weapon, extra magazines and, what's this, Bryce thought, the car keys! What luck! This was *far* too easy. He almost felt bad. It felt like stealing candy from a baby. He chuckled to himself and ran around to the driver's side of Geneviève's car forgoing the door and jumping right in. He searched her purse briefly and as he had hoped, her car key fob was in her purse. He put it in and pressed the start button as Drakkar and his men exited the house. Evie's car engine roared to life. Bryce gunned the engine and peeled out of the driveway in a cloud of dust and smoke waving to Drakkar and his remaining men as he turned the corner giving them the universal sign of his middle finger as he raced down the street.

Furious, Drakkar ordered his men to pick up their fallen comrade and throw him into the back seat. As they all piled into the vehicle, he realized the car's key was missing.

"Who has the key!" he demanded. "Who has the goddamned key!" he screeched again. All of his men glanced back at the unconscious Tito sprawled in the back seat. The others frantically searched Tito's pockets and came up empty. Drakkar made an enraged sound that struck fear into the hearts of his men. Screaming and cursing them with his every breath. Needless to say, Tito never regained consciousness. Drakkar pulled out his gun and shot Tito in the head several times. "Put that trash in the trunk!" He ordered angrily. Then he looked at Erik. "Get us out of here!"

Once they were out of range and Bryce knew for sure that they were not being followed, he pulled out his cell phone and placed a call to the one person he knew he could trust, Pierre DeGaul. Pierre DeGaul was Geneviève's oldest brother and Bryce's best friend. They had been friends since childhood, growing up together and now working together. Pierre allowed Geneviève to live pretty much alone in her island home now because he knew that Bryce was right next door and would keep an eye on her. Geneviève, of course, did not know that she was being quietly protected. If she found out, there would be hell to pay and Bryce and Pierre knew it. But, now, with all that was currently happening, he knew for sure their decision for him to purchase the house next door and shadow her covertly, had been the right decision, her temper be damned.

Chapter Six

On the mainland in sunny Los Angeles, California, Pierre DeGaul was enjoying an afternoon cup of coffee while taking in his ocean view. Use to his solitary lifestyle, he plodded through a crossword puzzle and sipped his coffee basking in the salty sea air and sunshine. Like his baby sister, Evie, Pierre loved the sea and all it had to offer. He was an avid surfer and fisherman in his spare time. "Spare time," he thought morosely, "what the hell was that!"

Folding his paper and settling it on the table, he methodically planned out the rest of his week. He was the head of his family's private security division. That also entailed organizing the private security for his family and that was a huge and sometimes challenging responsibility, especially when it came to securing Geneviève's safety. She was inclined to disappear at times. Strong willed and fiercely independent, she definitely gave him a run for his money. She was one of the few people that was not only able to match wits with him but was actually able to outsmart him too! On more than one occasion when she was a teenager, she had slipped away undetected. Pierre always found her, but the fact that she could slip away galled him. Their

Papillion, their butterfly, had slippery wings he laughed to himself. But this time, he thought to himself, he'd finally outsmarted her. He'd procured a puppy for her. Being the animal lover that she was, he knew she wouldn't be able to resist it. She'd always wanted a dog. So, on her birthday two years ago, he'd presented her with one of Míchel's pups from Sasha's litter. He'd absolutely had ulterior motives and they both knew it. But, to his relief, she'd accepted the pup and, as he predicted, they'd become inseparable. Now, he could relax, somewhat anyway, when it came to her safety. And, he was supremely confident that Bryce Marten, his best friend and right hand man in his part of the DeGaul business empire, would keep her safe and out of trouble. Smiling to himself, he decided it was time to resume his day. As he began to get up to go inside, his cell phone rang. He answered on the first ring when he saw the caller ID.

"Bryce, my friend, how the hell are ya!" Pierre answered jovially. But before he could get another word in, Bryce began talking. Pierre sat straight up in his chair listening intently. "What? When? Is she ok? Were either of you hurt? Where's Serge?" Pierre listened closely as Bryce relayed the morning's events. "Get to the airport Bryce. I'll have her jet waiting for you!" Pierre said. He was on full alert now.

"We're on our way there now Pierre." Bryce answered. "Have the jet readied but not the pilot or crew. At this point we trust no one but those in our inner circle. I'll have Bernard and Lucy with us."

"Agreed." Pierre said. "Let's rendezvous at The Clubhouse."

"Good idea! Pierre…" Bryce said warningly. "It's was Drakkar."

Pierre cursed creatively. "Hurry!" They disconnected.

Pierre needed to make two very important phone calls. First, and foremost, to the airport where Bryce was headed with his sister to make sure all the necessary preparations would be made according to his strict instructions. Then, he had to call his father. This call was the one he dreaded the most. He hated worrying the old man, but it had to be done. If Andre DeGaul found out his baby girl was in trouble and Pierre kept it from him, all hell would break loose. So, it was much easier to inform him than experience his wrath. The man was like Zeus on high with lightning bolts and far worse when it came to Evie.

Pierre called the airport where Bryce and Geneviève were headed and gave the specified instructions to Evie's pilot and crew member. Then, he secured his phone line, cringed and hit the speed dial button programmed for Andre on his phone.

Andre DeGaul answered his secure phone on the second ring sounding a bit groggy. Semi-retired now, he enjoyed the occasional nap.

"Père!" Pierre said urgently. "Geneviève is in trouble!"

"Where has she run off to this time Pierre?" He replied untroubled.

"No! Père, wake up damn it! Geneviève is in trouble!" The urgency in Pierre's voice got his full attention. Now fully awake, Andre DeGaul sat straight up in his bed.

Pierre had his full attention as he relayed the situation to his father. Andre listened intently, growing more and more anxious as each of Pierre's hurried words were spoken.

"Where is she now?" he interrupted.

"On the way to the airport, she's with Bryce. Père… Pierre hesitated. "It's him. It's Horus Drakkar!"

Andre DeGaul launched into a tirade of curses and threats that made Pierre wince. When he was finished he barked at his son to get his ass in gear and meet them at the agreed rendezvous location and speak to no one about what happened. Andre would call Míchel himself and he strictly forbid Pierre to tell his mother anything.

"I want to keep this from her as long as possible. Make sure that all our security details are tripled!" Andre ordered. "And, Pierre…" he paused and spoke in a dangerously soft growl. "Be careful son!" Andre disconnected their call.

Chapter Seven

Racing down highway fifty-six towards the airport, Bryce was doing some fast thinking. He had questions and he needed some answers yesterday. He glanced at Geneviève, who was seated in the passenger's seat next to him. She was still out cold. He pulled her cell phone out of her purse, and then put it down. A thought occurred to him. Why had they taken the time to bring her purse? He dumped the contents into the center console and began going through them. Just as he suspected, there was a transmitter in one of the pockets hidden in a packet of gum. He wouldn't have noticed it if it hadn't been blinking. He tossed the entire pack from the car watching it bounce on the pavement behind them in his rearview mirror. The car behind them ran it over and that was that.

He picked up her phone again and speed dialed Bernard. Bernard picked up on the first ring.

"Oui Miss Evie. We are on our way back now and your brute…"

"Bernard!" Bryce cut him off. "Turn around and head for the airport, now! Call Lucy and tell her to do the same. Do not go to the house! Understood?"

"Oui…of course Bryce!" Bernard replied, alarm clearly in his voice.

"Secure your phone before you make the call to Lucy and tell her to do the same before you relay any information to her." Bryce gave Bernard the specific instructions for both of them to follow to the letter.

"Absolutely, we will meet you there in twenty minutes."

"Bernard" Bryce said cautiously. "Be extremely careful and make sure you are not being followed."

"Oui! I will take every precaution I assure you. I taught you remember!" They disconnected.

Bernard called his wife over a secured line and told her what to do. She was still at the market so he stopped there and picked her up.

"What's going on Bernard?"

"I'm not sure Luce. But whatever it is, it can't be good if we're leaving the island."

"We're leaving the island? What's happened Bernard?" Lucy quickly put the groceries in the trunk of the car, slipped into the passenger's seat and secured her seatbelt. Sergeant was whining and pacing the backseat turning from window to window, sensing that something was very wrong. He was trained to read body language and his favorite humans reeked of apprehension. Lucy, realizing that Serge was in the backseat, shot an incredulous look at her husband. "Why isn't Serge with Evie?"

"He had his annual veterinary physical and shots today Luce. I volunteered to take him for her so she could enjoy her breakfast and her workout. We were only going to be gone for a couple of hours, if that long."

"Oh my God, Bernard!" Lucy exclaimed. "Evie!"

"I know Luce. If anything has happened to her, I will never forgive myself."

Bernard headed the car towards highway fifty-six and the airport.

"Bryce is with her now. I have complete confidence in his ability to keep her safe. We'll know more about what we are up against when we get to the airport."

"You're right, of course, as usual Bernard. But you know me, I'm a consummate worrier."

"Yes dear, I know."

"What the hell is going on?" She said wearily more to herself than to him.

"I don't know Luce. I just don't know."

Sergeant was still pacing in the back seat. He was on high alert reacting to the tension in the car. At times, he stood blocking the view of the rearview mirror.

"Serge" Bernard commanded. "Wo-sha!" Serge dropped immediately in compliance to a sternal position. But he did not give up his whining and Bernard didn't blame him. He was worried too. Lucy turned and spoke to the big dog in a soft voice to calm him down.

"It's ok boy. You'll be with your mistress soon." She scratched him behind his ears and under his chin. He calmed and quieted but remained on alert.

"C'est Bien." She crooned. "C'est Bien."

Chapter Eight

Bryce drove straight through the private entrance of the airport to the DeGaul's personal hanger. The DeGaul's had an entire fleet of Gulfstream jets. Geneviève's was a G150. The smallest of the Gulfstream airplanes, it has a wingspan of just over fifty-five feet and a total body length of almost fifty-seven feet. The little jet's maximum range of three thousand nautical miles was plenty to get them to their high mountain rendezvous location and small enough to land at the tiny airstrip that their hide-a-way destination maintained. It could accommodate six to eight passengers, including the crew, easily and was outfitted with a plush, extremely comfortable interior. It had eleven oval-shaped windows, a forward galley and an alt lavatory. Everything she would need for a comfortable flight anywhere she wanted or needed to go. However, its crew of two had been relieved of their duties for this flight. Bryce would pilot the plane and ferry them all to safety. Bernard and Lucy would resume their normal routine of looking after Geneviève while the flight was in progress.

He parked inside the hanger on the left of the airplane and met the pilot with a firm handshake and a polite greeting.

"Greg" he said inclining his head as he shook the man's hand.

"Sir. She's all fueled, prepped and ready to go per Mr. DeGaul's instructions. Nancy and I are to sit this one out. Mr.

DeGaul was very insistent. Have a safe trip. All that's left to do is file your flight plan."

"Will do Greg, thanks! You and Nancy have a great time on vacation. Bryce smiled and shook Greg's hand again.

"Thanks. We will."

He watched Greg jog to the other side of the hanger and slip into his tiny silver sports car and drive away with a wave. Bryce waved goodbye feigning no urgency. Once Greg was out of sight he ran over to the passenger side of Geneviève's car and began to unbuckle her seatbelt. Just as he was bending over to lift her out he spotted Bernard and Lucy's car speeding toward him. He stood and waited for them to enter the hanger.

Lucy was first out of the vehicle followed by Sergeant at her heels and passing her. The dog ran straight to his mistress and began barking furiously. Lucy caught up to the dog and grabbed his collar and leashed him. Giving Bryce a tearful look, she asked, "Is she ok? Is she hurt? What's going on Bryce?"

"We don't have all the details yet Aunt L. Please, get yourself and Serge aboard the plane."

Lucy began to choke on her words trying desperately not to cry. "I was at the market. I was only going to be gone for an hour at best."

"Don't worry about that now Tante. Grab whatever groceries you bought and load them too. Stow everything and get you and the dog secured. We're leaving as soon as I get Evie aboard and secured."

Bernard, who was standing just behind his wife gave Bryce a knowing nod and ushered his wife to the plane. "Aupie Serge" he commanded. Serge complied reluctantly. Bernard loaded his wife and the dog onto the plane and went back for the groceries and Evie's purse. Bryce carefully lifted Geneviève's inert body out of her car and up the few steps into the Gulfstream. He sat her gently into one of the leather captain's chair next to Lucy and turned to man the cockpit. Lucy strapped her in. Bernard secured the airplane's door then he sat in the co-pilots chair across from Bryce and secured his seatbelt.

"Tante Luce, will you look after her once we take off? I'll let you know when we reach our cruising altitude."

"Oui, of course! You know I will. Is she ok?"

"She's fine. Just out cold. Her vitals are all normal."

"Oh thank Goodness!" Lucy said with visible relief. "I won't pepper you with questions right now. I know and trust that you know what you are doing and that we will all be safe." She said with a watery relieved smile.

The Gulfstream had already been prepped and was ready to go. As soon as Bernard was onboard and the plane's door secured, Bryce radioed the tower and received the go-ahead for take-off. When he reached their cruising altitude of 41,000 feet, he gave Bernard the details of the situation.

"What's going on?" Bernard inquired in a tight soft voice. He didn't want Lucy to overhear their conversation.

"The threats to the family have just come to fruition." Bryce replied in an equally hushed voice.

"Damn!" Was Bernard's only response. He was contemplating the morning's events. It had started out as such a beautiful and peaceful morning. "What's the situation Bryce?"

Bryce filled Bernard in on the morning's events. When he finished, Bernard's face was flushed with anger, and something else Bryce couldn't quite identify. Fear, maybe? He was quiet for a long moment before he spoke again. "I assume we are headed to the Clubhouse?"

"You assume correct." Bryce answered. "Pierre is meeting us there. He should have a vehicle or two there by the time we arrive. The cabin's phones are secure and no one but the family knows about that place."

"Yes, I know." Bernard answered with a devilish grin. "Andre and I designed and built it ourselves."

Bryce stared at him with knowing eyes. "Yes, I know, with our help, Oncle." He wanted to ask what his real connection to Andre DeGaul was but decided this wasn't the time or the place for such inquiries.

"We need to know who the hell is behind all this mayhem." Bernard said through clinched teeth.

"Agreed. We may need your contacts and expertise on this one Oncle." Bryce said. "I don't think we'll have to blow your cover and expose you, but we're definitely going to need your connections."

Bernard swung his head around to look directly into Bryce's eyes, surprised at the seemingly nonchalant statement that just slipped from Bryce's mouth. "You seem pretty sure that I have connections and a cover to blow." He stated flatly with one eyebrow raised.

"Oncle Bernard…" Bryce began with only a slight edge of feigned irritation in his voice. "Pierre and I are not stupid by any means. You taught us just about everything we know about everything there is to know regarding combat situations, weapons, several different martial arts disciplines, the list goes on and on. We concluded a long time ago that you were no ordinary Marine like you claimed to be. We know that there is probably a hell of a lot more to it and for some reason, probably a very valid one, you haven't told us the whole story. We figured, if and when you wanted us to know, you'd tell us. Otherwise, it was on a need to know basis and we didn't need to know."

Bernard sighed. "Damn it all to hell. I told your father this day would come. You boys are just too smart for your own good. When this ordeal is over, we will explain everything." He picked up the plane's secured satellite phone and began to dial. He needed to talk to Andre.

"Bernard! Bryce! Evie's waking up." Lucy exclaimed.

Bryce and Bernard tabled their conversation for later and Bryce turned the controls over to Bernard. He made his way into the interior cabin of the little airplane while Bernard made his phone call.

Chapter Nine

Andre DeGaul was stepping out of the shower when his cell phone rang. He briskly made his way to the counter and answered it before it went to voicemail. "Speak…" He commanded when he answered.

"It's me, Zeus." Bernard replied. Zeus was Bernard's nickname for Andre. "I think we may have a big problem."

"I think you may be correct. I don't think we'll be able to maintain your cover or your secret for much longer." Andre agreed.

"Family meeting?" Bernard asked.

"Yeah, I think it's past time. I believe we have no choice at this point. The situation has made it unavoidable." Andre stated on a sigh. "I think you should prepare yourself mentally for her to be, shall we say, angry?"

"I think, brother, angry just may be the biggest understatement ever."

They fell into a momentary silence, both men contemplating how to handle the situation. "We'll need everyone together when we tell them. Are you involving Alexis?"

"HA!" Andre responded humorlessly. "You act like I have a choice?"

"You're right, of course. She's going to have our heads for this depending on how Evie reacts. You do know that, right?" Bernard said, resigned.

"I know, I know. Fortunately, for me anyway, it's your butt in the sling more than it is mine. We both apprised her of the situation years ago and she agreed. So, we may be safe. But you know she will side with Evie." Andre warned.

"Yep, I'm toast. Family meeting it is. My past has finally caught up with me. I'm almost positive I know who's pulling Drakkar's strings." Bernard stated with dread in his voice.

"Me, too Bernard. Me, too…" Andre sighed. We'll be there before dinner and we will bring Alexis' Beau, too. They were both resigned to the inevitable as they disconnected.

Sitting at the bar of his hotel on the big island of Hawaii, Horus Drakkar contemplated what he would say to his employer about how he'd lost Geneviève. Once they had acquired a new vehicle they made their way to the airport then on to the main island. He knew the element of surprise was gone. The DeGaul's now know that he is involved and that their precious little butterfly was the target. His employer will be most displeased about the element of surprise being thwarted, but would insist on pressing forward until he got what he wanted. Drakkar made it a point in his business dealings never to ask the questions, "Who? Or Why?" He didn't care. As long as his fee was paid, the devil himself could be his employer.

He'd recognized the man that rescued Geneviève. Bryce Marten. He knew him as a long time friend and family member of the DeGaul family. The Martens were part of the DeGaul's inner circle. He knew the history between the two families. He knew their secret. He also knew that without the element of surprise, this job just became that much harder. He considered, for a fraction of a second, ending his involvement, but knew that Bryce had seen and recognized him. Maybe, he thought wryly to himself, maybe if he could manage to kill both Bryce Marten and Pierre DeGaul in the process, this job just might be worth it. He could satisfy his employer and himself at the same time. His cell phone rang.

"Drakkar" he answered.

"Do you have my package Monsieur Drakkar?"

"No I do not, I'm afraid. It was not unattended as you had said it would be." He answered while assessing his well manicured hand.

"Hmmm…not unattended you say. I'll have to speak to my intelligence department and find out what went wrong. In the meantime, do we know where it was relocated to?"

Drakkar, already bored with the conversation said on a sigh, "No we do not have that information as of yet. Perhaps your intelligence department can be of some assistance and let us know?" he replied sarcastically.

"Perhaps." His employer replied. "I'll get back to you on that." Then he disconnected.

Drakkar had his own intelligence gathering underlings. He would find them eventually. The main problem in this situation was that the DeGaul Empire was vast. They could hide her just about anywhere in the world. This meant it was going to take a hell of a lot of manpower and time to dig up anything accurate on them. He was also aware that they had a vast number of hideaway places as well, ones that no one knew about. This was going to take precision and patience. A grin began to spread across his scarred face. He loved a challenge. "Let the games begin." He said to himself.

Chapter Ten

Situated on the south shore of Eagle Lake, in the beauty of the undeveloped Lassen National Forest, the DeGaul Clubhouse was the perfect place to hide. Lassen National Forest is located in northern California where the Sierra Nevada Mountains, the Cascades, the Modoc Plateau and the Great Basin meet. Inside the interior of the forest there are lava tubes and the land of Ishi, the last survivor of the Yahi Yana Native American tribe.

Eagle Lake is located at the meeting point of four major geologic regions. The Sierra Nevada mountain range is to the west and south which were formed by tectonic elevating along the edge of the continental plate. The Cascade Mountains are to the west and north and run through California, Oregon and Washington into Canada. This originally volcanic mountain range was the result of a collision between the Pacific and continental plates. Eagle Lake's location is inside the Great Basin. The semi-arid lands of the Modoc Plateau lie to the east. Long ago, the entire region was home to several different tribes of Native Americans. These tribes included Mountain Maidu, Hat Creek, Valley Maidu, Pit River and Paiute. All of these natives fished and hunted at the lake.

The lake itself was created by glaciers that melted during the last ice age. It is the second largest natural lake in California covering more than twenty-two thousand acres and boasts a shoreline that is over one hundred miles long.

The DeGaul's lakeside cabin was nestled on the south shoreline with a view of the lake and mountains beyond from the front and surrounded on three sides by matured trees. Three levels of decking all lead to a beautifully calm lake front setting. The cabin was approximately thirty miles north of Susanville and about one hundred twenty-five miles north of Reno, Nevada. Best of all it was accessible by plane. The lake also possessed a tiny airstrip for light aircraft to land. The scenery was exquisite and the location was extremely secluded which was the reason why Andre DeGaul and Bernard Cartier had chosen it. No one could trace the cabin. It was completely cut off from the outside world. It was totally off the grid. This place did not exist on any map. It was designed by the two men and erected by all the men in the family with some technical help from the CIA. The house was equipped with state-of-the-art high-tech electronics and securities systems and everything in it was undetectable and untraceable. It was the perfect safe-house.

Chapter Eleven

Geneviève thought she heard voices. Her head was screaming with a pounding headache and she had a weird nasty taste in her mouth. The voices seemed familiar and gentle, but the last thing she remembered was a big burly man restraining her and blacking out trying to scream and fight. She began to cry. Tears welled and fell from her eyes as she began to fight the arms that began to restrain her. She opened her eyes but all was a blur. She was disoriented and afraid.

Bryce stood over Geneviève gently but firmly holding her in her seat. She was fighting him with all her might. He decided to take a different tact. He picked her up and sat down in her seat. Placing her gently in his lap, he spoke softly into her ear.

"Evie…It's ok. You're safe now? He said gently.

"Open your eyes Chéri." Lucy crooned softly while stroking her hair. "Please Evie, open your eyes. You're safe now."

Geneviève's eyes began to focus. Two familiar faces came into view. She immediately stopped struggling. "Where am I? What happened? My head hurts. I think I may throw up." She said suddenly.

Lucy was prepared and handed her a bag for such an occasion. Geneviève heaved into the little bag, her body racking with each wretch. Bryce calmly held on to her until the episode was over. Lucy made her way to the galley and returned with a glass of ice cold water.

"Sip this Chéri. The sick will pass." Lucy said soothingly.

"What's going on?" Geneviève began to cry again. Bryce turned her face into his shoulder and let her weep. He stroked her back and her hair. He kissed her forehead and whispered to her. When she seemed to relax and her crying jag was subsiding, he lifted her face to look at her.

"You're safe now Evie. We don't have all the details yet, but here's what we know thus far." Bryce told her everything. He felt he needed to in order to make sure she wouldn't pull one of her disappearing acts.

"This man is after me? Why?" She asked with a look of incredulity.

"That's what we have to find out, Evie. We don't know yet so I need you to promise me that you will not pull one of your disappearing acts on us. This time, Evie, there really is someone after you." Bryce was searching her puffy grey-green eyes looking for hints of that defiance she was famous for.

"I promise." She finally said with a sniff and a sigh. "I promise to be good."

Everyone in the little plane breathed a sigh of relief including Bernard who had been listening to the events going on in the cabin behind him. The cockpit was open so he could hear everything. Listening to her cry and feeling every bit of her vulnerability made him even angrier. He would kill the man that dared to threaten her.

In the background, Geneviève heard a familiar sound. It had always been there but she hadn't paid attention to it nor had she recognized it until that moment. It was Serge. He was whining and digging at his kennel door. She left the security of Bryce's lap and arms and, on wobbly legs, made her way aft to Serge's carrier. She released the latch and let him out. He just about knocked her over when he burst from the kennel and began furiously licking her. Geneviève, through her haze of dizziness and nausea, let him lick her hands, arms and feet. She nuzzled, cooed and scratched him. It was then that she realized she was still in her bathing suit. "I'm still in my swim attire! Geez!" she said disgusted. "My peaceful morning ruined!"

She turned to look at everyone who was, in turn, looking at her. They were watching her while she and Serge greeted one another. Lucy had a look of concern on her face, but Bryce had a peculiar smirk on his face.

"What?" she inquired. "I know that smirk Bryce Marten! What's so funny?"

Bryce cleared his throat. "Ummm…Nice view!" he said playfully.

Lucy realized that he was referring to the fact that Geneviève's back had been to them initially and she was still wearing her thong, without her sarong. Lucy gasped and punched Bryce's shoulder.

"Avert your eyes ya big pervert! Get your butt back up to the cockpit and see if Bernard needs you! Go on!" She shooed. Turning Bryce and pushing him forward towards the cockpit.

Bryce turned, looking over his shoulder as Lucy pushed him, for one last look at Geneviève's perfect little butt, but she had already turned to face him. Her cheeks pink with embarrassment. She scowled at him. He laughed and returned to the cockpit and took up his seat. Lucy returned to Geneviève and guided her to the restroom which was aft in the little aircraft.

"Come along Chéri, let's see if you have a change of clothes aboard." Lucy found Geneviève's small stash of clothing stowed in a cabinet across from the lavatory.

"Here, put this on." Lucy handed her a pink silk Chanel sundress. The little dress was mid-thigh in length and had thin shoulder straps that crisscrossed in the back. Lucy also handed her a pair of delicate deep purple kitten heeled sandals to put on. Geneviève took the little dress and sandals into the bathroom.

"I need to clean up Tante Luce. I haven't showered from my swim in the ocean. I feel salty." She said.

"I understand. Clean up and I'll make us all something to eat."

"Thank you Tante." Geneviève smiled.

Closing the door, Geneviève grimaced when she caught sight of herself in the little lavatory mirror. She was a mess. Her hair was all over the place and she had salty streaks down her cheeks from her crying jag and the ocean. "You look like hell!"

She said to herself as she began the task of putting herself right again.

Once settled in his seat, Bernard gave Bryce a knowing look. "When are you going to tell her? He said questioningly.

"Tell who, what? Bryce replied still chuckling.

Bernard sighed shaking his head. "When are you going to tell Missy how you feel about her?"

Bryce stiffened then looked at Bernard. "How do you know how I feel about Evie?"

Bernard burst out laughing. "We *all* know how you feel about her! It's written all over you every time you're around her."

Bryce sat ridged in his seat, contemplating. After a long moment of silence and listening to Bernard's laughter, he finally spoke up. "Does Evie know, too?"

"No, we think she's still oblivious."

"Who is *we*?" Bryce asked disbelievingly.

"Everyone in the DeGaul's inner circle." was Bernard's only response.

The DeGaul's inner circle consisted of the DeGaul family members, Andre, Alexis, Pierre, Míchel and Geneviève, of course, but it also included some of their extended family as well. Bernard and Lucy and their two children, Andre's five brothers and two sisters and their spouses and children and Alexis's two brothers and her sister and their spouses and children made up the DeGaul's inner circle. The Marten family was included, too, but upon his parent's deaths, Bryce was the only one left to represent them. He had no siblings and both of his parents had been only children. It was left up to him to pass on the Marten name.

"Am I that transparent?" He asked dumbfounded.

"Yep. I'm sorry but you're as transparent as glass. Don't worry about it son." He patted Bryce's shoulder smiling widely. "It was all part of the plan."

"Plan? What plan?" Confusion was evident in his voice.

"Lunch is ready!" Lucy appeared with two plates in her hands. "I made sandwiches. You have a choice of barbeque or plain potato chips. There is also a choice of beverage which includes, milk, juice, root beer or water." She finished with a smile. "What will it be boys?" she inquired.

Bernard, thankful for Lucy's impeccable timing, spoke up first. "I'll have barbeque chips and root beer please."

Bryce, distracted by the food said, "I'll have the same Tante Luce. Thank you."

"Coming right up gentlemen." She said cheerfully. She left the cockpit and returned moments later with their chips and drinks in hand. They ate companionably. Each man lost in his own thoughts and the view of the vast mostly clear skyline preceding them.

Geneviève emerged from the bathroom feeling much better. Her hair was wet and in a loosely braided ponytail. Her face was freshly scrubbed and she had applied some light makeup that simply enhanced her already beautiful features. She felt so much better on the outside, however her insides were in knots. Why was someone after her? For the first time in her life, Geneviève was afraid. She was still a little dizzy from the sedative that she had been given and more than a little nauseous. But she was also hungry and her stomach began to grumble its protest. She stumbled, but Lucy was there beside her in an instant to stabilize her.

"Sit down Evie. I've prepared you a small sandwich. It's your favorite, turkey and bacon with pepper jack cheese and all your favorite condiments. I even purchased your favorite root beer today while I was out shopping, Henry Weinhart's." She said with a smile.

"Merci Tante, you are too good to me." She said as Lucy guided her back to her seat.

"I know Chéri, I know." Lucy put Geneviève's plate in front of her and encouraged her to eat. Then she sat down beside her and began to eat her own sandwich. Serge, evidently feeling left out, began to whine and lick his chops.

"Oh Serge." Geneviève said laughing. "You're such a beggar! Just pitiful!" They laughed at him and tossed him bits of turkey.

Bernard broke the silence when he said, "We're almost there."

"I'll start making the landing preparations Oncle B. Why don't you go back there and get the ladies ready for landing." Bryce suggested.

"Good idea. I'll take the dishes with me." Bernard replied cheerfully. "I want to see how my Missy is doing anyway. I'll be back in a flash."

Bernard left the cockpit with the lunch dishes and emptied root beer bottles in tow. He found the ladies already in their seats and fastened in.

"Ladies..." He said with a smile. "I trust you are enjoying the flight." His words being more of a statement than a question, Bernard leaned down to kiss his wife lightly on her lips and then he kissed Geneviève on her forehead. They both answered in unison.

"Oui, we are thank you."

"How are you feeling Missy?

"Much better Oncle B. Tante Luce is a healer don'tcha know." She said placing her hand over Lucy's.

"Oh oui, I am all too familiar with her healing capabilities." He said with a smile and a wink. "We are almost to our intended destination. I was sent back here to make sure that you ladies were all seated and secured. I see that you are, so I will return to my post. I'm so very glad that you are unharmed Ms. Missy." Bernard kissed her cheek then turned to secure Serge. He returned to his co-pilot seat in the cockpit, secured himself in and began his portion of the landing procedure.

"I assume the women are all tucked in and ready to go?" Bryce queried.

"That they are." Bernard replied. "We're just about ready to land this little bird. Are you ready over there?"

"Yes, I will be releasing the landing gear in five minutes." Bryce acknowledged.

"Roger that. I'll call the tower and relay our approach." Bernard replied.

Both men had their eyes and attention focused on the horizon and the plane's controls. They were preparing to land. Their final destination was coming into view and they were guiding the small plane into its final approach.

Chapter Twelve

Pierre was standing at the end of Eagle Lake's tiny airstrip waiting for Geneviève's Gulfstream to land. He and Míchel had arrived an hour before and made all the security preparations to the safe house. Pierre watched as the small plane made its final approach and landed lightly on the tiny runway. It taxied to a stop, and, with the help of the Eagle Lake landing crew of one individual, they secured the plane and waited for its occupants to emerge. The door was unsecured and let down and everyone on board began to make their way down the stairs.

Geneviève and Serge were the first ones to exit the plane. Pierre wasted no time getting her and the dog into the first of two

BMWs that were there waiting with their engines running. He opened the passenger door and the rear door simultaneously to allow them both into the vehicle. Evie put her seat belt on and Serge settled down on the back seat. Lucy was next to exit. She was carrying most of the groceries that she had previously shopped for with her. Pierre kissed her on her cheek, took the groceries from her and settled her into the car with Geneviève and Serge.

"I'll be right back, ladies." He said. He placed the groceries in the trunk and trotted back to the plane. Climbing its short staircase, he entered the cockpit where Bryce and Bernard were busy shutting down the plane's engines and console.

Pierre greeted them with a smile and informal handshakes. "Welcome back to Eagle Lake gentlemen. I have a car for you waiting on the tarmac." Pierre motioned to the vehicle waiting for them. "Hurry up and get all your gear so we can get everyone out of sight. I have a crew on standby waiting to take the plane out of here and hop scotch it across the globe just in case someone is tracking our air traffic. They won't suspect anyone off loaded here because it was the farthest this little plane could go without refueling. Anyone tracking will assume just that. You refueled and continued on. No one would ever suspect that you would stay here because it's too remote and out of the way. They would deem it an unsafe place to hide and of course look elsewhere which is exactly why we chose it." They all exchanged knowing looks.

"Will do." Bryce answered. "Go ahead and get the ladies situated. We're right behind you. I know my way there. Bernard and I will grab our gear and follow you back. Oh… and grab the rest of Lucy's groceries or she'll make us drive all the way back here to get them. By the way, you do know that once they see the house, the cat will be out of the bag, literally, right?"

"Okay. Good idea! You're absolutely right about Aunt Luc! She would definitely make us drive back for her groceries. And, yes, the proverbial cat will be out of the bag big time. I'll just tell them the truth. I think they can handle it." Bryce paused thoughtfully. "Of course, we may never get to have another *man vacation* again though." They all laughed. Then Pierre hesitated before asking, "How's Evie?"

Bernard answered this time with a somewhat edgy tone of voice. "She's…" He hesitated thoughtfully, "She's shaken. She'll recover. My Missy is a strong lady, but her world has just been turned upside down. We won't be able to keep her contained for very long, you know that Pierre. She'll feel like we're being overprotective and overbearing again."

Pierre sighed. "I know Oncle…I know. She may surprise us this time though, especially since there really is someone after her." The smile on Pierre's face did not reach his eyes. "Míchel is here with me and he's waiting for you in the second car. I'll see you both shortly."

Pierre exited the plane while Bryce and Bernard gathered their gear and exited behind him. He crossed to the vehicle where Geneviève and Lucy were waiting, inclined his head in Míchel's direction then got in. "Shall we go home now ladies?" Lucy answered yes, but Geneviève simply nodded her head.

They all rode in companionable silence for awhile as Pierre guided the car along the windy highway. Neither of the ladies had ever been to this home hidden in the mountains. They hadn't even known it existed. The scenery was breathtakingly beautiful. Geneviève rode in the passenger's seat next to Pierre and took it all in. While he drove, Pierre patiently kept the silence. He knew his sister well and knew she needed the quiet and her relaxed body language told him that she felt safe. She was in "decompression mode" as she called it. She would likely sequester herself in her room for awhile until she came to terms with the events of the last twenty-four hours.

In the second car, Míchel, Bernard and Bryce were all involved in a discussion about how the ladies were going to react. None of them doubted the women's ability to handle the situation. They were more concerned about their hides. This location was not known to anyone but the men in the family and they knew that there would be hell to pay. The women in their family had fiery tempers.

"Do you think he's told them yet?" Bryce said chuckling.

"Hell no!" Míchel answered. "I don't see him ducking and dodging yet."

They all laughed.

Bernard spoke up next. "You boys do realize that we left him to take the brunt of all the heat from those two, don't you?"

"Damn straight!" Bryce and Míchel said in unison.

"Better him than us." Bryce said.

"So, you're thinking that he will endure and we will get off scot free?" Bernard asked with an arched eyebrow.

"Are you kidding? We're all going to have our asses handed to us when this is all over. Tante Luc is going to skin us alive." Bryce replied both worried and amused.

"Well, I don't know about you two, but I'm a bit more concerned about my mother." Míchel added.

"Well that's easy son." Bernard said with an easy grin. "She's simply going to kill us all!"

They all laughed again.

"I spoke to your father, Míchel. He and your mother will be arriving this evening by car. As chance would have it, she returned from the gallery in Milan yesterday. They are already on their way here. Poor bastard has to break the news to her and ride in the car with a mad and worried female. They are bringing Beau with them too." Bernard finished.

"Good. Bryce said approvingly. "The more canines we have patrolling the perimeter the better. Did you bring Sasha, Míchel?"

"Oui, I did. She's already patrolling the house." He answered.

"Excellent. Then we are well covered for security. Nothing and no one will get past them or us. We will all be safe here."

The men rode the rest of the way planning and strategizing. All of them were totally aware of the danger that seemed to be manifesting itself and completely confident that anything and everything would be handled. The safe house was fully stocked with everything they could possibly need for self defense and survival. They were all extensively trained in both defensive and survival tactics thanks to their Oncle B. He taught them a plethora of other things too, some the boys suspected were super secret things but never questioned. As both cars approached the unmarked road they soberly continued to strategize about how they would keep everyone safe while they figured out what the hell was going on.

Chapter Thirteen

Pierre slowed the vehicle as he approached the main roadway to the safe house. Evie couldn't see the house from the main road. She broke her silence asking, "Pierre is it much farther."

"No Evie. It's about five minutes up this road." Pierre replied.

"This road is unmarked?" She inquired.

"Oui, it is unmarked and not on any map, anywhere. This house doesn't exist. Only a handful of people know its location and they are all here right now except for Père. It's totally self-sufficient and off the grid. It's powered by the latest technologies of solar energy and windmills."

"How is that possible Pierre? Someone had to construct it. There had to be a construction crew. I'm guessing hundreds of people know this place exists. Something like this cannot possibly be kept a secret…it's imposs…." She broke off as the house came into view. "…ible" she finished, awestruck. "Wow!" She whispered.

From the back seat he heard Lucy whistle. "Ditto! What she said!" Serge, sensing that the ride was ending, sat up. Pierre stopped the car in the expansive driveway and let his little sister take in the view. It was spectacular and he never got tired of the views himself.

The house was perfectly nestled in the pines almost hidden. There were huge boulders that seemed to loom over the walkways to the entrance. There was a small courtyard with lovely patio furniture that blended into the background of the house. On the left of the courtyard was a stone pathway that led to the entrance. The front of the home had a stone facing and gabled roofline. The windows were expansive. It felt so inviting and welcoming, surrounded by breathtakingly beautiful snow capped mountain peaks.

"Evie." He said gently, breaking the spell she seemed to be under. "Evie look at me."

Geneviève tore her eyes away from the spectacular scene to look at her brother. "It's overwhelming and gorgeous, but I don't think we'll be safe here Pierre. Why did we come here?"

"Evie. Remember I said only a handful of people know this place even exists."

"But…" Evie began.

Pierre gently cut her off but placing his index finger over her lips. "Let me explain. The reason I know that only a handful of people know about this place is because myself, Bryce, Oncle Bernard, Míchel, Rogét and Père built it. We personally brought in all the equipment, etc. and built it."

"How? When? She was stuttering with a stupefied look on her face. In the back seat, Lucy's face was just as confused and inquiring.

"Remember all those vacations the men took together?

"Oui. The ones where you all said that it was for male bonding time or something ridiculous like that. Which by the way, we figured you were up to something, but you always returned home with fish, so we decided that you may have actually been vacationing."

"Yes, well, we did do some fishing here and there or at least one of us did until we caught something. We couldn't have the women following us. You know how you are." He chuckled just a little nervously. "We kept its existence a secret from everyone because the fewer people that knew about this place the safer it would be in the event we needed to be off the grid."

Lucy piped in from the back seat, "Remind me to smack Bernard in the back of the head. In fact, I think I owe all of you a good smacking."

"Anything for you Tante Luc." Pierre grinned. "Shall we go inside now ladies?"

The second car parked behind them and they all began to exit their vehicles. The women got out slowly taking in the view while the men worked efficiently to get everything out of the vehicles and into the house. Míchel emerged from the house after taking in the groceries and made his way down to them. Serge spotted Sasha and dashed out of the car and across the courtyard. They greeted one another with yelps and happy barks. They, too, were related. Serge was Sasha's pup and pick of the litter. They worked well together and made a lethal team. They were the pride and joy of the DeGaul's security branch of operations. Once everything had been unloaded and everyone was making their way into the house, Míchel watched the two dogs with pride. He'd been the one to train them as he did all the dogs in their operation. He was in charge of that part of their security division. Pierre was the CEO of the Security branch overall but Míchel was in charge of the breeding and training program of all their dogs. He had a natural way with animals so his position fit him perfectly.

Rogét and Míchel greeted Evie with a warm hug and a kiss on her forehead. She accepted and returned their greetings with a kiss on each of their cheeks. Then both men turned and greeted

Lucy with equal affection and ushered the women inside. Lucy, glad to see her son, gave him an extra kiss on his cheeks.

"Bonjour my son." She patted his cheek.

"Bonjour maman." Rogét answered and kissed her cheek again. Then he left them standing in the expansive foyer with Míchel and joined the other men in the situation room which was tucked away on the other side of the house.

Without turning to look at each other, Geneviève and Lucy began to speak to one another.

"Tante Luc...did you know about this place?"

"No Chéri I did not and since you are asking me the same question I was going to ask of you, I think it's fair for me to assume that you really didn't know about this place either."

"No Tante, I didn't." They stood in silence for a few more moments. Lucy was first to break the silence. "I'm going to smack them all!" She said in a quiet firm voice. Then they began to explore the house.

Míchel, seeing his opportunity to flee before the women remembered he was standing there with them, slipped down an adjacent hallway before he was noticed.

The men were all holding a short strategy meeting while they had a moment alone without the women listening. They were all leaning over Rogét's shoulders peering at his computer monitor until he put the information up onto one of the three the giant wall monitors mounted directly in front of them.

"Is there anything or anyone on the monitors Ro? Were we followed?" Pierre inquired.

"No, nothing so far. The only things the cameras are picking up are the dogs making their rounds around the perimeter."

"Did you have time to stock up the supplies before we arrived?" Bernard chimed in.

"Oh Oui, Oncle. We are fully stocked and armed to the teeth." Rogét answered.

"Excellent! Now what do we tell the ladies." Bryce asked the room with a raised eyebrow.

At that moment, Míchel entered the room and answered him. "I don't know, but whatever you're going to do, you'd better do it fast because Tante Lucy has promised us all a smacking!"

"Damn…any ideas? Bryce asked the room.

"Ummmm…how much time do we have?" Pierre asked desperately.

Laughing nervously, Bernard answered, "not much, they are making their way down the hallway towards us as we speak."

They all glanced at the monitor that featured the cameras in the hallway.

"No worries Oncle. I've got this one handled." Rogét answered smugly. "Gentlemen, watch me work."

The ladies entered the doorway of the situation room and stood in awe. It was a massive room with three giant monitors on the west wall, book shelves and cubbies on the north and south walls and the entire east wall was nothing but windows. The view was spectacular. It overlooked the lake and the mountains on the other side. There were several desks strategically positioned around the room so that each one had a view of the window and the monitors. The entire room was lit up with natural light. However, there seemed to be no glare on the monitors from all the natural sunlight.

"Wow" both ladies said in unison. Then Lucy looked directly at her husband and glowered.

"Now Luc…" Bernard began. He took a step forward and stopped short when Rogét stepped smoothly between him and Lucy successfully cutting off her advance.

"Maman! My lovely queen, have you seen your suite yet?" He asked in a soft inquiring voice.

Lucy, taken by surprise, began to stutter. "Well no…well…I don't know… I'm…," she looked at Evie, "we're not sure. We're a bit lost I'm afraid."

"Tsk, tsk. Now we can't have that now, can we? Rogét crooned. "Please allow me to give you both the grand tour. I promise it will be worth it." He winked at both of them. "If you two gorgeous babes would each have an arm, I will be honored to escort you to your suites and be your grand tour guide."

Lucy, now completely distracted and disarmed by his charm and flattery, punched his shoulder playfully and took his arm. "Now you cut that out Rogét Cartier, you know flattery gets you everywhere with your mother. She chuckled.

Bryce stepped forward, "Rogét, if you don't mind, I'd like to escort Evie to her suite."

Míchel smiled and nodded. "Absolutely Bryce, be my guest." Bryce offered his arm to Evie and she took it. As they left the room, they did not see the knowing smiles and nods in their direction.

"The poor bastard is sunk." Bernard said.

"Poor sap. The worst part of it is that I think Evie is totally unaware of how he feels." Rogét said. "He's wearing his emotions on the tips of his fingers and she is completely clueless."

"Should we tell them? You know, in a round-about way. Anyone think they need a push? Míchel asked the room.

"Heavens no." Lucy said flatly. "They'll figure it out all on their own."

"Tante Luc is right Míchel. Don't ruin it for them. Pierre spoke up. "Besides, I don't think Bryce is ready for Evie to know because I don't think he's figured it out yet himself, not completely anyway."

"Figured what out completely?" Rogét asked.

"That he's in love with her Rogét." Pierre answered.

"How is that possible? Every time he sees her, he practically trips over his tongue!" Míchel said laughing.

They all chuckled. Then Lucy turned to her son and said, "nice try on the distraction angle, but I'm too quick for you. Your opportunity is lost. Your charm has worn off. Now scram! Bernard?" Lucy pinned her husband with one of her looks.

Bernard sighed. "Yes, dear. I know. I have some explaining to do. Son, if you don't mind, I shall escort my lovely wife to our suite. I promise to make sure she's happy so we can have dinner tonight since none of us cook!"

"She's all yours père." Rogét handed his mother over to his father. "Good luck and may the force be with you. Oh and we don't have to worry about cooking because Josie is here too. She rode up with me. She'll be doing all the cooking." Rogét stated with a satisfied grin.

They all laughed again. Then Lucy said, "Keep laughing boys and it will be air pudding and wind sauce for dinner! She's my daughter, remember."

Pierre and Rogét stifled laughs and tried to act shamed as Bernard and Lucy left the situation room.

Chapter Fourteen

Thousands of miles away, on a tiny secluded island in the Greek Islands northeast of Crete, Alkis Georgiou sat by his pool impatiently waiting for a communication from his hired assassin. He didn't want Geneviève DeGaul harmed in any way, at least, not yet. He wanted to take her from his enemy. Make her vanish from his life. He wanted to make him pay for all the wrong he felt was done to him. Pay for all the lies and deceit that surrounded him.

So he sat, and waited for the call that he felt would be the game changer. He waited for his victory in an uncompromising, menacing vigilance. He wondered if he would have to take matters into his own hands. He wondered if they had figured out who was behind the botched abduction. His opponent was a very smart and dangerous man. And, the element of surprise was lost to him now. They would rally around his prize, making this venture extremely difficult. But, he was supremely confident that he would, in the end, be successful. He would crush his enemy and leave him lost in the world without her.

Bernard Cartier was not who he claimed to be. It had taken Alkis quite some time to sift through all the bullshit to find out where his adversary had disappeared to. And, to his credit, Bernard had covered his tracks very, very thoroughly. His name changes made tracking him extremely difficult but at last he had found him. And the knowledge that his enemy had offspring… well that just made the situation even sweeter.

Alkis sat back in his chair and wondered how his prize would react when she learned her father's true identity as well as her own. It will be revealed and soon. He would make her his own. Keep her and use her for his amusement. And, when he grew bored with her, he'd deliver her cold, dead, rotting corpse back to her lying, double crossing father.

Geneviève was exhausted. She allowed Bryce to walk her through the expansive home toward what she hoped was her bedroom. All she wanted was a really hot bubble bath and sleep.

Bryce knew she was only humoring him so he kept the tour brief. He showed her where the kitchen was and how to get to the beach if she wanted to go outside into the backyard. There was an indoor pool and a jacuzzi she was welcome to use whenever she wanted to indulge herself. Ending the tour in front of lovely tall carved oak double doors, Bryce handed Evie a key.

"This is your suite Evie." He said in a low voice. "I know you're tired and probably more than overwhelmed by the today's events."

"I am Bryce, utterly exhausted." She said with weariness in her voice. "I don't understand what's going on or why." Afraid she might start crying again, she took the offered key and opened the door to her suite. It was absolutely gorgeous. In the center of the room was a king sized canopy bed with soft flowing material covering it. The interior of the room was decorated in bold rich colors of reds, blues and emerald greens. The wall facing the lake was entirely glass made up of floor to ceiling windows. The view was spectacular. There was crown molding trimming the room and rich Brazilian cherry hardwood floors. In front of the window wall was a sitting area with a red chaise lounge chair and two very comfortable looking puffy club chairs. Between the chairs was a small coffee table with a vase of fresh red roses. There was beautiful bold abstract artwork on the walls and two giant fluffy doggy beds for her four-legged companion. In the bathroom there was a deep fuchsia glass vessel sink with an intricately delicate floral design etched into the surface of the glass. Acres of earthy toned marble counter space, a vanity, jetted soaking tub, a huge stand alone shower, big enough for three people, with a rain shower head and multiple wall mounted shower heads.

Bryce stood in her doorway and watched her go from room to room touching various objects here and there. She was use to luxury true enough but this room had been unmistakably and specifically designed for her. Turning in his direction, she finally spoke.

"This was decorated with me in mind wasn't it?"

"Yes it was." He replied.

"Even the clothes in the closet are all my size. Who designed it? Do you know? She asked feeling overwhelmed, again.

"Yes, I do know…"

When he didn't offer anything more, she asked again. "Who designed this suite for me Bryce?

Somewhat reluctantly, he answered "I did Evie."

She looked at him then. "You did?"

"Yes." He replied sheepishly. Trying not to show his nervousness he asked. "Do you like it? I tried to put everything in here that I thought you'd like and need. I worked very closely with a decorator and she gave me very good advice, however, the true test of my success was for you to see it and approve of all that I had done."

"It's beautiful Bryce, absolutely serene and gorgeous!"

For a moment, they simply stared at one another. Geneviève thought she saw more than just curiosity in his eyes. She looked around the room and then back at him. Then she kissed him on his cheeks and said with a warm smile and a girlish giggle, "Merci. I love it." Curious now she asked, "Who was the designer that helped you? I may need her to design some of the rooms in my home too."

Before Bryce could answer her Josephine breezed into the room and answered. "I helped him! Although, I was completely unaware that it was for this room. "I..." she emphasized, "...was told it was for your bungalow at your parent's house. It was passed off as being a big birthday surprise." She stood in the doorway, hands on hips, glaring at Bryce. "Bryce Marten you lied to me!" She said feigning anger. "You owe me big time, Monsieur!"

"Ummm..." Seeing his exit blocked for a quick escape with her standing in the doorway, he started doing some fast thinking. He figured he'd pass the buck in this situation and put all the blame on Pierre, but before he could say anything at all, Geneviève pushed him aside to give her cousin a big hug.

"Josie!" Evie exclaimed in surprise. The two women embraced in a tight affectionate hug. "I can't believe you're here too!"

"Yep. They dragged my ass to this place too. They seem to be under the misconception that I'm going to do all the cooking since I'm a world renowned chef and all." She winked at Bryce and cut her eyes towards the door giving him the opportunity to escape. He mouthed a "thank you" and slipped out of the room closing the door behind him.

Bryce was more than happy to be out of the hot seat. He made his way back to the situation room where Rogét, Míchel and Pierre were still putting their heads together.

"Anything new?" he asked.

They all turned in unison and looked at him with knowing smirks on their faces. Míchel slid his hands into the front pockets of his jeans and began to rock back and forth on his heels. "Well, yes…but that can wait. We're more interested in what you have to say." He stated with a smile on his face.

Feeling like he just jumped out of the frying pan and into the fire, he stared at the faces staring back at him expectantly. Deciding to play ignorant he said flatly, "I have no idea what you're talking about."

"Like hell you don't!" Pierre challenged. "I'm your best friend. Spill it!"

"Spill what?" Bryce verbally side-stepped that question.

"Every man in this room knows you are head over heels for Evie. Did you tell her how you felt? You were certainly gone long enough to, and if you didn't tell her when she saw her suite she should have figured it out."

"Yeah, what he said!" Rogét added.

"Well shit! Am I that damned obvious?" He asked scrubbing his hands over his frustrated face.

"Yep!" they all said.

"I'll take that as a no. Pay up you fellas. I told you he wasn't ready." Pierre said holding his hand out to each man.

"No freakin way!" Míchel said laughing. "I'm not paying you one red dime until I get an answer straight from the horse's mouth. So to speak, of course, I'm not calling you a horse… a horse's ass maybe… but not the whole horse." Again they all laughed.

"Well…" Pierre inquired with an eyebrow raised. "Did you?"

Bryce paused to stare at them in disbelief. "No, no I didn't you sorry sons of …"

"Bryce Marten! Don't you dare finish that statement!" Lucy exclaimed, smacking the back of his head. "Now I'm sure you gentlemen have something else to do besides harass and torment this poor love sick man." Lucy turned to smile and wink at him.

Bernard entered the room behind her and gave Bryce a sympathetic pat on the back. "Listen up gentlemen. Mr. and Mrs. DeGaul are on their way here. They should be here any minute and Andre has called a family meeting." The room fell silent. All laughter and joking ceased and Bernard had everyone's attention.

"I don't have to tell you that there is something really dangerous going on. I will tell you, however, that there is a great deal more to this story. Evie will need us all. That's all the information I can give, for now. You all need to get rested and cleaned up. We will meet after dinner."

They all exited the situation room and headed for their individual suites.

Geneviève stood staring at her cousin Josephine in wonder, delight and disbelief. Josephine was Bernard and Lucy's only daughter and the two women had grown up together. She was a world renowned chef and Evie's best friend. The two women embraced once more.

"How did you get here? When did you get here?" Evie asked.

"I came with Rogét. He picked me up on his way here. Told me it was some big emergency and didn't really give me a choice. He had already called ahead to my house and had Giselle pack me a bag." Giselle was Josephine's personal assistant. She made sure Josie stayed on schedule. "On my way here, I had to rearrange my entire schedule for "to be determined" because he wouldn't give me any information on when I'd be returning. I brought Apollo with me. Everyone is on lockdown. Your parents are on their way."

"Oui, I know. They did inform me of that much. I don't understand why this is happening to me Josie." Evie sat down on her bed and gave her friend the rundown of all that she knew thus far. She told her everything that had happened prior to them arriving there at the house. Josie stood in shocked silence as she listened to the details.

"Oh Evie…" she said finally. Sitting next to her on the bed she said, "It's probably a good thing that you were out cold for most of the ordeal. I can't imagine how frightened you must have been."

Evie was not prone to crying jags but there she sat tearing, again, she thought. This day has just been overwhelming. Josie, seeing that the retelling of the day's events was still upsetting Evie, placed an arm around her shoulder and gave her cousin a little squeeze.

"Let's get you into that big soaker tub. I'm sure you'll feel better after a soak and some food. I'm headed to the kitchen now to whip something up." Josie said smiling.

"Everything you need is in the bathroom Evie. Relax for awhile. I'll come and get you when dinner is ready."

"That's probably a good idea. I couldn't wash the salt out of my hair or off my body on the plane. Thanks Josie." The bussed each other's cheeks and Josie left her room and closed the door behind her.

Chapter Fifteen

Just south of Susanville, California, Andre and Alexis DeGaul were making their way north on highway 395. There hadn't been much in the way of conversation between them because they both knew that this particular family meeting was going to be an intense one. They both were feeling the guilt of keeping the family's secret all these years. A family secret that was so dangerous they had had no choice but to keep it in order to keep everyone safe and out of harm's way, until now.

How? How did someone find out the truth? Only four people knew the truth and two of them were in the car together right now. Bernard was the only other family member that knew the truth and his best friend was the fourth person. None of whom would ever jeopardize the health and safety of the family. She had her suspicions about Pierre knowing the truth since he would have been old enough to remember everything, but he had never questioned or even brought up the subject, so she just wasn't sure. And, even if he did know, he certainly wouldn't be the one to let the secret out. This was going to be a nightmare. Alexis pondered these thoughts as she rode in silence in the passenger's seat next to her husband.

He cleared his throat before he spoke. "Are you going to be silent for our entire ride Lexy? I know I should have told you where we were going before we left, but I felt it best that I didn't, that way you couldn't accidently tell anyone where we were going or why. I did tell you as soon as we got on the road though. Doesn't that count?"

Sighing she answered, "Andre I am not angry with you anymore. You know that I don't hold on to anger for very long. I am not sitting over here sulking. I'm worried."

"Worried? I'd ask why, but then that would be a very stupid question. However, I will ask you this, which part of this very ugly situation are you worried about the most?"

"I'm worried about Evie and her safety. I'm worried that she may not take what we have to tell her very well. I'm worried about the effect that this will have on our family as a unit. I'm worried about all of it Andre…all of it. "

"There was nothing we could have done differently Lex. What was I supposed to do? Ignore the needs of a family member? Would you in that situation? Could you?" he spoke gently, yet somewhat exasperated.

"You misunderstand Dear." Alexis deliberately calmed her voice in order to ease the tension between them. "This isn't about you or me or even Bernard. This is about Geneviève. I expected you to be there for him. I wouldn't change anything or any decision we made then or afterwards. Family takes care of family. We are supposed to support and protect one another. That's what we did. I just hope that Evie can forgive some very big white lies."

"I'm sorry Lex. I jumped to conclusions too soon as usual." He gave her a wry smile and said, "I know, I know…I'm a hot-head."

"Yes you are dear. And, I wouldn't have you any other way."

Andre picked up her left hand and lifted it to his lips to kiss her knuckles lightly. "So, you're not angry about the house in the mountains? He asked cautiously.

"Again, you misunderstand dear." She said with a smile. "I am furious about that house. And, the fact that you kept it a secret from me all this time has your butt in a very tight spot with me. However, I have put that on the back burner for now due to the fact that there are much more urgent matters that need to be dealt with and tended to. I will, however, address that in the future and take it out of your hide later."

"Yes dear!" he said smiling at her. "My hide will be severely skinned I'm sure of it."

"Not to change the subject, but how much longer before we arrive? We've been on the road for hours. I understand why we couldn't fly, but my butt is beginning to complain!" She said wriggling in her seat. "Beau is restless too." She turned to see her canine companion watching her. Beau was her four-year-old German shepherd and Sergeant's sire. Alexis traveled nowhere without him.

"It's not too far now. We have maybe an hour and Beau is fine."

"Well…in that case…I'm going to rest my eyes and mind. I'm feeling a bit weary and if we are revealing things over dinner, this is going to be one stressful evening and I'm already tired."

"No worries." He said evenly. "I'll wake you when we get there."

Horace Drakkar's plane landed at LAX that afternoon. Since he did not travel with luggage he skipped the baggage claim area altogether and slipped into the awaiting car outside the area's doors. Erik was driving. The rest of his men all traveled separately and at different times. Erik was his right hand man and always traveled with him personally.

"Do you have any information for me Erik?"

"They left the island by plane as you suspected. It flew as far as it could before refueling at a tiny airstrip north of Susanville in California. We are still tracking it."

"Good. I want to know when and where that plane stops and stays." He paused thoughtfully for a moment, "As a precaution I want a team stationed at or near every place they go. Just in case they get off the plane somewhere and they just keep it going for us to chase. Plant teams in Susanville and Reno."

"Yes sir. Consider it done." Erik pulled out his cell phone and made his calls. As instructed, he had teams dispatched towards both Susanville and Reno. Then he gave orders for two man teams to be sent to every city that Geneviève's little plane landed in for any reason.

Satisfied that his second in command had control of the situation, Drakkar relaxed.

"Where are we staying while here in L.A.?" He asked Erik casually once he was off the phone.

"Your suite at the Ritz-Carlton in Marina del Rey. That part of town is closest to the airport just in case we need to leave quickly. I took the liberty of calling your personal assistant Tiffany. I informed her when we were scheduled to arrive and gave her the parts of your itinerary that I was already aware of."

"Of course you did." Drakkar replied seemingly indifferent. "Thank you. It's close to LAX and therefore convenient." Advise the men joining us here that I want everyone downstairs at the bar by 6:00pm sharp. I want a full update at that time."

"Yes sir. It will be done. Shall I make a reservation for all of us?"

Drakkar thought for a moment then replied. "No, make the reservation for just me, plus one. We will have our meeting in the bar area. I will be having dinner with Sophie."

"Yes sir." Erik turned into the driveway of the hotel and parked leaving the motor on. The doorman opened the passenger side door and Drakkar stepped out and walked into the hotel towards the front desk. A valet driver opened Erik's door simultaneously and Erik got out, handed the young man a fifty dollar bill, and followed Drakkar into the building.

A petite young lady in her early twenties was waiting for them to approach the desk. "Good afternoon, Monsieur Drakkar. Glad to see you with us again. I trust your flight in went well?" She said cheerfully greeting them with a charming smile.

"Ahhh…Mademoiselle Tiffany." He said, inclining his head slightly. "Still beautiful as ever I see. Yes, my flight was without complications or delays. Is my suite ready my dear?"

"Of course, Monsieur. I made sure it would be after I received the phone call from your associate regarding your arrival itinerary. I made sure that housekeeping freshened up your corner suite." She said lifting her chin in a proud posture and smiling at him."

"I don't even know why I ask such questions." He said, with a faux sigh. "You always take such good care of me." He winked at her.

Suite 1310 was his private suite. He paid for it indefinitely to insure that no one else would have access to it and that it would remain available upon his return to the city.

Their conversation remained light and playfully flirty while Tiffany completed the check-in process. She was fast and efficient and he appreciated her special care and accommodation. He was in Los Angeles often and stayed at this very hotel each time. And, since he was a frequent visitor of importance and status, he was accommodated by the same person each time he stayed there. Tiffany was his personal assistant at the Ritz-Carlton. She did everything for him while he was onsite and made all of his arrangements and accommodations that pertained to the hotel. She made sure his meals were delivered to his suite at the appropriate times if he was eating in or she made all of his reservations at the restaurant there inside the hotel or any other outside venue. He tipped her very, very well and kept that just between them.

She handed him his key cards and he handed her his signature gilded envelope embossed with the letters "H" and "D" containing her tip usually in ten crisp new hundred dollar bills. Anytime he visited, Tiffany received no less than eight to ten of these gilded envelops.

"For you, Mademoiselle." He said taking her hand and kissing her fingers lightly.

"Merci, Monsieur." Tiffany blushed. "All of your arrangements for this evening's dinner have been made. You and your party have the corner booth in the bar area as requested at six o'clock and your dinner reservations for two have been made for seven."

"Merci, Tiffany. I will let you know my itinerary for the week." He gave her a smile and then turned to Erik who had been standing to the side all the while. As they began walking towards the elevators, he said. "You will be staying in the second bedroom as usual in my suite." He handed him the second key card to his suite. "See to it that the rest of our party is at the bar promptly at six. I am going up to shower and change before dinner."

"Yes sir. I will make sure the men are in our usual adjoining suite and they understand what's to be reported."

"Good. Thank you Erik." He said dismissively. Erik turned and headed back towards the front desk as Drakkar pushed the button for the floor to his suite.

Chapter Sixteen

Geneviève opted for a long hot shower instead of a bath. She washed her hair and just stood for awhile among the shower's jets that were spraying her with hot water from almost every direction. She bathed and stepped out into the steamy bathroom. She wrapped herself in a giant heated body towel and stepped towards her vanity. She sat down and assessed herself in the mirror. Her hair was wet, her eyes seemed haunted and puffy from all the crying she'd done and she just didn't recognize the person staring back at her. That was an image of some scared little girl, not the feisty independent woman that she saw herself as.

"Enough!" She said to the image in the mirror. "I don't know what's gotten into you but I have had enough. Pull yourself together and act like you have some sense."

Good pep-talk she thought to herself. She picked up her brush and began untangling her curls. She decided to leave her hair wet and let it dry naturally. She didn't feel like wielding her blow dryer or curling iron at the moment. She just didn't have the energy. So she added her leave-in conditioners and put her hair in a loose ponytail. Her bangs were too short to fit into the ponytail and springy curls framed her face and neck. She added light makeup to her face to rejuvenate her tired features. Satisfied now with the image of herself looking back at her, she got up from her chair and went to her closet to find something appropriate and comfortable for dinner at home. At home, she thought. This was home? Apparently so, even though it had been a complete secret from the women in the family, it was still a home that she could see would accommodate all of them very comfortably. Then, another thought struck her curiously. Bryce had had a hand in designing her accommodations. A big hand in fact, he'd designed it primarily on his own. Not her brothers, but Bryce. That was certainly unexpected. The fact that he had accommodated just about all of her tastes in style and wardrobe was a little unnerving. Well, on second thought, Josie did say she helped too, so maybe, she helped more than she let on. Bryce couldn't know her that well, could he? She would table those thoughts for another day. Ready to once again face the world she dressed and left her suite headed for the kitchen.

She found Josie in the kitchen with Lucy, both of them immersed in conversation and food. Without missing a beat, Lucy handed Geneviève a glass of Muscato wine in a crystal wine glass and continued on in conversation and cooking.

"How are you feeling Chéri?

"Right as rain, Tante, thank you for asking." She said with a genuine smile.

"You had me worried." Josie chimed in. "You almost never cry Evie. I am so sorry this is happening to you. Well, to us really. What happens to one of us happens to all of us. You know our family motto." She said smiling while she squashed garlic out of the garlic press she was using.

"It smells heavenly in here. What are you two cooking?"

"Comfort food, of course! You were upset, so tonight's dinner is all about you Evie!" Josie said with a smile. "I'm fixing your favorites."

"Favorites?"

"Yep." Josie replied.

"Well that implies more than one…?" Evie said curiously.

"Oui it does. Can't get anything past her can we maman? She said to Lucy pretending to ignore Evie.

"No dear, she's a smart cookie."

"I'm right here you two!" They all laughed.

"Well…ok then…how many of them are you making?" Evie inquired, even more curious now.

"How many do you have? Lucy asked.

"Well, you know I love your fried chicken Tante Luc!"

"Check!" Josie said, pretending to check off an imaginary air check list.

"With your famous garlic mashed potatoes and green beans, too?"

"Check, and check!" Josie checked off her air list again continuing to cook.

"Lasagna?"

"Check!"

Dumbfounded Evie asked tentatively, "Jambalaya?"

"Check!...again! Ding! Ding! Ding!" Josie teased.

"Is she toying with me Tante Luc. I'm asking you now because I know Josie. She'd tease me relentlessly if she thought I'd believe her!"

"No Chéri. Josie isn't teasing you."

"That's a lot of food Josie!" Evie finally said in disbelief.

"Oui, enough to feed a small army. Which is what we have just in case you hadn't notice, all of the men are here." Josie said evenly.

"Oh, my goodness, that's right! I was so lost in me I totally forgot about them!" Evie laughed out loud. "What do you need me to do?" Evie asked.

"Nothing at all, unless you're feeling up to it Chéri." Lucy answered before Josie could. Giving her daughter that mommy look before Josie had a chance to speak.

"What?" Josie replied innocently. "We could use some help here maman…just saying…just a thought." Josie retorted playfully sarcastic.

"Are you kidding Tante? I need to keep busy. Tell me how I can help."

"Alright Josephine, she's all yours!"

"Oh lord, what was I thinking?" Evie feigned regret.

They all laughed.

"You can make your corn bread Evie. You may want to triple your recipe though. It's one of the family favorites." Josie advised.

"I can do that! Evie smiled as she donned a lovely floral apron.

The women worked companionably side by side in the kitchen laughing, talking and cooking.

Down the hallway in the great room, just outside the dining room, all of the men in the family were gathered around the massive fireplace discussing the day's events and fine-tuning their plans to keep the family safe. The room was lavishly furnished with comfortable overstuffed chairs and a huge sectional that was positioned directly in front of the fireplace. It was shaped in a half circle so that each and every person sitting on it would have a view of the fireplace and the television above it. The slate wood burning fireplace was massive. It took up most of the wall being almost six feet long. Bryce and Pierre were getting it started when the front door opened and Andre and Alexis DeGaul entered the Foyer. All the men went to greet them. They all kissed Alexis's cheeks and gave her a hug. Andre shook all their hands as they passed by to collect their bags from them.

Pierre greeted his parents. "You know the way to your suite père." He said, as they shook hands. "The ladies are in the kitchen maman, if you'd like to join them."

Before she could ask, Michel was by her side. "I'll give you the grand tour maman." He said, smiling down at her. Alexis was a petite five foot four and weighed about one hundred twenty-five pounds. She had the same grey-green eyes that Geneviève had. Her hair was the same honey color as Evie's too, but with more wave than curl. She looked up at her six foot two son and smiled.

"Alright Míchel, show me the way!"

"My pleasure." He said offering his arm. "This way if s'il vous plaît, madame." They left the crowded foyer and headed towards the direction of the kitchen. Míchel played the perfect tour guide as he pointed out and named all of the common areas as they passed them on their way down the hall.

Watching them leave Andre spoke to Pierre. "Has our situation changed?"

"No sir, nothing has changed. The dogs are patrolling the perimeter of the estate and everyone, except the ladies are aware of the family meeting that you have called. They are prepared to listen over dinner."

"Good, good." Andre thought for a moment longer before adding, "Slight change in plans…" he said slowly, thoughtfully.

"Oh? ...ok? What would you like to change? Pierre asked him.

"Well… I'm thinking about changing the time and location of this discussion. I need to speak to Bernard first, however, but I want to have the meeting after dinner in the great room. Everyone will be somewhat relaxed with all the food I know Josephine is preparing in that kitchen. I can smell it from here." He said ruefully. "I'm starving! Your mother wouldn't let us stop to get something to eat. She kept saying it would ruin dinner and I wasn't going to challenge her considering I was already in the hot seat about the house."

"Yeah….how did she take that little bit of news?" Pierre asked wincing.

"I don't know, she hasn't made me pay for it yet. She was too concerned about all the other things that were going on."

"Hmmm…I'd say you got off lucky old man!" Pierre slapped his dad on the back as they made their way out of the foyer and into the great room. "I'll let the everyone know about the changes."

"Thanks son, where's Bernard?" Andre inquired.

"He's in the situation room. He cleared us all out of there so he could make some phone calls to his some of his contacts. He's trying to piece this situation together." Pierre answered.

"I'll leave him to it then. He'll join us when he's finished I'm sure." Andre said smoothly. But, he thought to himself, his past really is finally catching up with him.

In the situation room, Bernard was teleconferencing with an old friend.

"I've got a situation Mal. I need your help." Bernard ran down the day's events to his long time friend and former spec ops partner, Malcolm Divine.

"That's a shitty deal you've got going there. Someone besides me knows who you really are and that's a very big problem." Malcolm said, frowning thoughtfully. He leaned forward in his chair. Let me do some digging and I'll get back to you. In the meantime, don't surface anywhere until we figure this thing out. Keep a tight rein on that Evie. She's a pistol and when the smoke clears she's gonna be pissed. God I love the fiery women in your family!" He smiled then soberly said, "I'll get back to you as soon as I can."

"Thanks, Mal. I appreciate anything you can do or find out. I think we're on borrowed time at this point. We need to know who we're dealing with and eliminate the threat to my family." Bernard said gravely.

"Agreed. I'm on it." Malcolm replied. "I'll see what I can dig up. Sit tight and I'll talk to you soon."

They disconnected. Bernard left the situation room and headed for the great room. He'd seen Andre and Alexis's car pull up in the driveway on the monitors. He needed to talk to Andre, alone. But first, he'd make a pit stop in the kitchen and see how the ladies were holding up.

Geneviève was taking one cast iron skillet of cornbread out of the oven and replacing it with another. The women were working in their respective areas and chatting companionably. A question was formulating in Evie's mind and she was curious to know if the other two ladies had the same question. "Hey! I just thought about something, Josie." She said with one delicate eyebrow raised. "What's going on with Bryce?"

"What do you mean?"

"You know what I mean. How is it that you helped him design a room for me, here, in this house, of all places? Another thought occurred to her, "Did you know about this place before today? She asked inquiringly.

"No. I had no idea this place even existed. Bryce told me that he was painting a picture for you and wanted to know what your room would look like if you designed it. He made me promise not to tell you because it was supposed to be a big surprise. I knew about a painting not this house."

"He paints?" Evie and Lucy asked in surprised unison. They all laughed.

Josie, realizing that she let the cat out of the bag, answered reluctantly, "Oui, but don't you dare tell him that I told you."

It was Lucy's turn to be stunned. "Is he any good? And, if he is, how come I don't know? He could be featured in Alexis's galleries!"

"Merde!" Josie said under her breath.

"Language, young lady!" Lucy admonished.

"Sorry. I'm as useless as a leaky refrigerator when it comes to secrets!" Josie said exasperated.

Evie piped in, "Well you might as well spill it since you've already let the proverbial cat out of the bag. Don't leave us hanging here in suspense Jo!"

Raising her eyes to the ceiling, Josie ushered them closer and spoke in a hushed voice. "He *IS* featured in Tante Alexis' galleries maman! Remember the artist she can never seem to get to make a personal appearance for an opening?"

"Monsieur Papillon? The mysterious artist that only speaks to her directly via email or through his personal assistant and never seems to show up at any opening she's ever given for his work? She inquired. "Not the artist that I have personally purchased some of his works because of their breath-taking realism?

"Oui, that's the one. Monsieur P.M. Papillon, her mysteriously shy artist. Some of his works are here in this very house."

"Oui, but what does the P.M. stand for Josie? Lucy asked shocked.

"Pour Mon, maman." Lucy's mouth dropped open. "Shut up!" she said waving a hand then pressing it to her chest, "Really?" They both turned and looked at Geneviève.

Feeling a bit self-conscious with them both looking at her with seemingly knowing eyes, she said, "What? Why are you looking at me?"

"You know what it translates to Evie!" Josie said smiling.

"Yes, of course I do. It means For My Butterfly…so?"

"Oh my God! Mére, please school your niece on men…!" Josie said throwing up her hands laughing. "…because I give up!"

Lucy stared at Geneviève for a moment, assessing her reaction. Then a wide grin spread across her lovely face. "You really don't know do you Chéri?"

"Know what?" Evie said exasperated. "What don't I know?"

"Wow!" Josie said shaking her head. "You are the dumbest smart woman I know!"

"Wait for it…" Lucy said. "I can see her wheels turning. What's your middle name Chéri?" Lucy prodded gently.

"Papillon… OH… MY… GOD!" The realization of what they were saying hit her like a ton of bricks.

"Better grab her maman, I think she's gonna fall over." Josie said teasing. "Like I said, the dumbest smart woman I know." She turned to stir the pot of Jambalaya.

"Tante? …wow! Ok…so he paints for me." Evie took a deep breath and let out a nervous laugh. She was flushed and completely embarrassed. "You're right! I am the dumbest smart person you know!" She finished. She was about to pump them for more information when Bernard entered the kitchen.

He stopped in the doorway and assessed the women who all turned to look at him.

"Am I interrupting something ladies?" He asked noting Evie's flushed face. "Are you ok Evie? You look as though you're going to fall over from shock."

"Oh no père, you're right on time, she's fine. Just some embarrassing girl talk is all." Josie said winking at her father.

"Uh… ok… well I stopped by to get a report on the progress of dinner. I know the natives must be getting restless with all the wonderful smells emanating from this kitchen. You three sure know how to torture us." He said smiling and sniffing the air around him. He reached for a piece of the cornbread and Lucy smacked his hand with her wooden spoon.

"Ouch!" He cried pulling his injured hand back.

"Out of the kitchen you! Tell the *natives* dinner will be ready in about a half hour so they need to wash up and make themselves presentable." Lucy said sternly. "Go on now! We won't be showing you any favoritism."

At that moment Alexis and Míchel entered the kitchen.

"Mére!" Evie rushed to embrace Alexis as did Lucy and Josie. Bernard seeing his opportunity to snitch a piece of cornbread laughed and left the kitchen headed for the great room through the dining room. As he expected, as soon as he emerged from the dining room the rest of the room began asking about dinner.

"Are they done yet?" Bryce asked.

"They are…" Bernard began to explain but was cut off by Rogét.

"Yeah, my belly button is touching my spine! I'm starving!" Rogét complained.

"Your belly button is always touching your spine Rogét." Pierre teased.

"This coming from the man with not one but two hollow legs which require regular fillings? Seriously?" Bryce retorted towards Pierre.

"Gentlemen!" That was all Andre needed to say to quiet the room. "Will you all please shut up so Bernard here can get a word in edge-wise about the status of the food that we are so anxiously waiting for."

"Thank you Andre." He said. "Before I was so rudely interrupted…" deliberately stalling for effect. "The goddesses of the kitchen have informed me that dinner will be ready in about a half an hour. If you are interested in eating, then you must clean up and make yourselves presentable before you enter their dining area."

"Woo hoo!" Rogét exclaimed. "Finally!"

"I am requesting that you boys do what you always do and set the table." Bernard added.

"Boys? What boys?" Pierre said teasing Bernard.

"You three young men. Better?" Bernard asked with one dark eyebrow raised.

"Well…" he started.

"Get your butts in gear boys, Zeus is hungry!" Andre voice boomed deeply. "Don't make me use my lightning bolts." He said laughing.

"Oh Damn, not the dreaded lightning bolts. Let's go fellas." Míchel said feigning fear. They began exiting the room. Míchel shouted as he retreated laughing from the room, "Violence is the tool of the ignorant Pére!"

"Yeah well dad's feelin' real ignorant right about now son, for several reasons." He said under his breath turning to look at Bernard.

"Yeah… Uncle is too." Bernard added.

Chapter Seventeen

Once the others finally cleared the great room, Bernard and Andre sat down in the big club chairs next to each other and leaned in close. They knew they only had a few minutes before the men returned to set the table and any of the women could walk in on their conversation, but they had to take that moment for this discussion.

"What did Mal say?" Andre asked in a hushed voice.

"He said he would do some digging and get back to me in a nutshell."

"Someone went through a lot of trouble to find you Vincent. We knew this day was a possibility and we built this house especially for this situation. Now that we're here, I'm not sure how we should proceed."

"We have to tell them the truth Andre. It's the only way to insure that everyone remains safe. They need to know everything."

"Everything?" Andre lifted a brow inquiringly.

"You know what I mean. Don't be a smartass! Missy needs to know now. It's time."

"You're right, of course." Andre sighed and sat back in the chair. "She does need to know. I just don't know how she'll take it all. I don't know how anyone is going to take it all. Are you planning to tell her why you won't call her by her given name?

Are you going to tell her why you call her Missy? Either way, this is all FUBAR!" Andre said resigned and disgusted.

"What's all FUBAR Pére? Evie asked. She was standing in the entry doorway of the dining room drying her hands on a kitchen towel smiling at them unsure and feeling as though she was interrupting. When they heard her voice, both men jumped to their feet.

"Nothing babygirl! I was just letting off a little steam with Bernard here." He glanced Bernard's way. "We were waiting for one of you lovely ladies to come out and tell us that the wonderful food we smell is ready for us to enjoy. Come here and give your père a hug. I haven't seen you in awhile. Are you ok?"

Geneviève immersed herself in her daddy's big arms. He always made her feel so small and so fragile when he hugged her. Compared to her, he was a giant but she fit perfectly in his arms and always felt safety, comfort, warmth and best of all loved. She was a daddy's girl after all, she thought.

"I'm fine Pére. Really, I am. I love the house." She said. "But I think maman and Tante Lucy are going to kill all of you. They are planning your demise in the kitchen." She gave him a stern look as she left the safety of his embrace. Bernard chuckled.

"Don't think you've gotten off scott-free Oncle, Tante Lucy is planning your demise too." She said sending him the same look she gave her father. "Both of you are in deep, deep doo doo."

"Damn and here I thought he would take all the blame." Bernard said ruefully.

"Hell no!" Andre scoffed. "Are you kidding man? I told you in the beginning, if I go down, you were going with me!"

They all laughed. Then Evie added. "Well you're both definitely going down. I wouldn't want to be either of you right now."

"Thanks Missy for that lovely vote of confidence." Bernard said sarcastically.

Pierre, Bryce, Míchel and Rogét all re-entered the great room. Evie brightened.

"Guess who gets to set the table?" She said smiling at them.

"Yes, we know. Zeus here has already commanded it." Pierre said pointing a thumb at his father.

"We're coming. We're coming. Sheesh!" Rogét added feigning protest.

"You always were a brat, Evie." Míchel said as he passed her and entered the dining room.

"It's all your fault Míchel." She retorted. "Out of everyone, you spoiled me the most!"

"Lies!" he denied. "All lies! Pierre spoiled you the most. It's entirely his fault!"

"Hey! I resemble that remark!" Pierre chimed in laughing.

Alexis entered the room carrying a serving platter with mounds of cornbread on it. "All of you are to blame. All of you spoiled her. Now suck it up and deal with her brattiness!" She said, joining in the banter.

"Thank you, maman. Finally, a voice of reason on my side that knows and speaks the truth about my brattiness." Geneviève sauntered out of the room into the kitchen. Josie stopped her in the wide doorway and handed her the platter of fried chicken.

"Who's hungry?" She shouted into the room smiling. "Dinner is served!"

Several hoots and hollers of joy came from the hungry men in the dining room as more and more food was set onto the dining room table.

In Los Angeles, Horace Drakkar was leaving his suite and headed for the elevator. Erik was by his side and they were having an intense discussion on how the meeting downstairs would be conducted.

"This will be a brief report, correct Erik?"

"Yes sir. I have chosen to bring in our two best men, the twins, Ian and Ivan. Ian has the tracking information you requested. They will trail us where ever we go and provide back up if we need it."

"Excellent."

They reached the bottom floor of the hotel and the elevator doors opened. As they moved across the lobby towards the bar area, two men got up from their seats.

"Sir." They said in unison as Drakkar and Erik approached.

"Ian, Ivan…" Erik re-introduced the men, "this is Mr. Drakkar."

"Gentlemen." Drakkar shook their hands.

"Shall we?" Erik gestured Drakkar into the entrance of the bar area. Standing just beyond the entrance, waiting patiently, was Tiffany. She handed him a manila envelope when his party approached.

"Good evening Monsieur Drakkar." She greeted him with her usual warm and pleasant smile.

"Mademoiselle Tiffany." He returned, kissing her hand lightly. He took the envelope from her as she spoke.

"I took the liberty of printing the itinerary you sent me so that you would have a hard copy of your schedule while you're here visiting our hotel."

"Merci mademoiselle, as always, you have made yourself indispensible."

"Merci Monsieur Drakkar, your booth is ready for you on the west corner of the bar area."

"We will find our way from here mademoiselle, merci."

"You are most welcome Monsieur." Tiffany turned to exit then turned back. "Oh, Monsieur Drakkar, I almost forgot..." she shook her head a little flustered. "Frances will be your waitress tonight. Lena is ill."

"Ah, yes, that will be fine. Merci, again, Mademoiselle." He answered over his shoulder.

They found their reserved table and sat down.

"Brief Monsieur Drakkar now Ian if you please, only if there is something new." Erik said.

"There is nothing new as of yet sir. The two teams we sent to the instructed destinations should arrive in both places late tonight or tomorrow morning. They will report directly to me at all times and in eight hour intervals twenty-four hours a day. I, in turn, will report to Erik what I know, and it is my understanding, that he will then relay any new developments to you."

Erik looked at Drakkar for confirmation.

"That will be fine. Until further notice, you will report directly to Erik. You both have your orders, yes?"

"Yes." Ian replied.

"Very well then, if there is nothing else to report, you are dismissed. Drakkar said without looking up from the papers Tiffany had handed him. The two men exited the table and moved to the bar. Right on schedule, Frances was making her way towards them smiling brightly.

She stopped at the bar to give drink orders and then made her way to their booth.

"Your table is ready Mr. Drakkar and your guest is already seated. Shall I order the salmon for you sir?"

"Yes, thank you Frances that will be fine." He said returning her smile.

"If you are ready, you may follow me now." She said pleasantly.

"We are." He said. Drakkar and Erik followed her to their table. Seated there when they arrived was Mademoiselle Sophie. She was a tall dark haired woman with flawless olive-colored skin.

She had expressive big brown eyes, high cheek bones and a luscious mouth that was currently wearing a sassy, sexy smile. She was wearing a sleek black dress that showed off her ample bosom and curves. Sophie Elise belonged to him and served as his companion when he visited Los Angeles. She was his arm candy when such occasions called for having a date and she served his physical needs as well. He kept her in the top floor penthouse of one of his buildings and allotted funds for her to spend. She stood and offered her hand to him as he approached.

"Mademoiselle Sophie. He said, kissing her hand. You are a vision for my eyes to feast upon."

Sophie smiled, "And, you are a shameless flatterer Monsieur!" She teased flushing with nervousness.

They sat. Erik remained standing and waited for Drakkar and Sophie to settle in before excusing himself to a nearby table with Ian and Ivan.

"What are we having tonight Monsieur?" She inquired. He always ordered for them both.

"I chose the salmon for you this evening my dear, your favorite." He said charmingly.

"Oh… Lovely. Wine?" She suggested coyly.

"Of course, if it pleases you." He answered.

He ordered a glass of Riesling for her and a dry martini for himself.

"Are you prepared for this evening, Sophie?" He said suddenly. Already undressing her with his eyes, Drakkar placed his hand on her leg and squeezed…hard. Sophie didn't flinch but felt the pain of his fingers digging into her thigh. She knew in that moment that he would not be gentle this time and braced herself for the night to come. She searched for comfort in her thoughts. She remembered her new friend. He was kind and sweet. She would confide in him as soon as she was able to get online again. He would listen to her without judgment and even offer his advice and support.

Chapter Eighteen

Dinner was lively as usual when the family got together. The men were riotous and the women their usual sassy and defiant selves.

"Who made this cornbread, it's horrible!" Pierre teased. "Bryce could you pass the cornbread man, stop hogging it!" He elbowed Bryce in the ribs.

"Horrible?" Evie shouted. "Choke, Pierre!" She laughed. "Don't you dare pass him another piece Bryce Marten or you won't get any more either!" Evie commanded.

"Damn, ummm… wow…, you're on your own man! The woman has me by the stomach." Bryce winked at Evie. "And, as you well know, I like to eat, so you're S.O.L.!"

"What? You're trading me in for food?" Pierre exclaimed feigning surprise.

Bryce raised his hands and hunched his shoulders in a helpless gesture.

"Pierre Francis DeGaul!" Alexis said sternly. "You leave Bryce alone before I get after you young man."

"Maman? You're taking his side?"

"Pierre…" Andre began in a calm matter of fact voice. "If I were you, I'd quit while I was ahead. There is no way you're winning this argument. None of us will side with you when it involves food! Have you lost your mind son?"

Laughter erupted and lit up the room. Everyone was gleefully picking on one another, bantering back and forth. This was normal dinner fun and they all enjoyed one another's company.

Once the dessert had been served, Andre took the opportunity to speak to his family. "I am requesting that everyone convene in the great room after dinner. I have something to discuss with the entire family."

The room fell silent as Andre spoke. Evie felt a strange sensation as her father's eyes fell upon her and lingered. He continued speaking. "I will ask that everyone withhold all questions until the primary information has been spoken and explained. I assure you that all questions will be answered."

Andre glanced at Bernard pointedly for a brief moment and Bernard acknowledged him with a tiny almost imperceptible nod of agreement. Evie witnessed the exchange and watched her father and uncle intently. She had a feeling that something was very,

very wrong. She started to be the inquisitive natured woman they all knew her to be, but changed her mind when Bernard looked her way and held her gaze. Andre had taken his seat and began to dig into the hot apple pie a la mode that was set before him as did the rest of the family. But for a moment that seemed more like an eternity, she and Bernard were locked in questioning stares. She could see the hesitation in his eyes but didn't understand it. He gave her a smile and broke their trance. She glanced around the table to see if anyone else was looking at her. No one else seemed to be paying her any attention. They were all engrossed in conversation and banter and the apple pie. She sighed and thought to herself that maybe she was imagining things, though she didn't truly believe that. She knew something bad was happening otherwise there wouldn't be an evil, dangerous, scarred man after her. Josie lightly kicked her under the table.

"What's that look about Evie. You don't like the pie?" She asked one dark eyebrow raised.

"No, no…" Evie said quickly. "I love your apple pie. You know that Josie." She smiled at her cousin. "I was thinking that I should just wrap it in Velcro and attach it to my hips!"

"Are you kidding??" Míchel exclaimed around a mouthful of pie and ice cream. "You're willing to risk not tasting all this deliciousness?"

"Well no, I…" Evie started to explain when Pierre interrupted her.

"Leave her alone Míchel, you pig." Pierre teased him. "Don't worry Evie, I'll eat it if you don't want it."

"Over my dead body!" Bryce spoke up. "I'm sitting the closest to her! That pie is mine!" Both men made a fork dash for Evie's dessert plate but before either of them could reach it, Evie grabbed her steak knife.

"If either of you value your fingers, neither of you will cross the edge of my plate lest you draw back nubs!" She spoke in a calm even tone with a look of death and destruction in her eyes. Both men quickly drew their forks back, laughing.

"Cheri!" Alexis exclaimed in a scolding voice from the other side of the table catching everyone at the table by surprise. "I taught you better..." She eyed the carving knife sitting on the edge of the platter and pointed to it. "Use that knife instead to defend your plate dear! No sense in chopping more than once. It's simply a waste of energy."

Everyone at the table roared with laughter.

"Maman!" Míchel said, feigning hurt. "Really?

"You always did take her side!" Pierre complained.

"Surely you wouldn't let her cut off our fingers with one of Josie's Wüsthof knives!" Bryce said plaintively.

Lucy spoke up this time. "If you enjoy your fingers on your hands where they belong boys, I would advise you to refrain from attempting to take anything off of Missy's dessert plate. As you all well know, she is quite handy with a knife. My Bernard has made it so." Lucy smiled affectionately at her husband and winked.

"So harsh, ladies. How did you put it Míchel, violence is the tool of the ignorant?" Rogét interjected.

Again, they all laughed.

After the dessert plates had been taken away and they were all finished eating, everyone began to make their way to the great room. Conversation was still lively and teasing. It had been a very long time since all of them had gotten together in this way. Andre thought to himself. It was unfortunate that it had to be under such circumstances. He took a deep breath and sighed. Looking at Bernard he asked, "Are you ready?"

"Indeed I am, as ready as I can be for such a situation. You were correct in saying that this situation is FUBAR!" Saying no more, they entered the great room to address the family.

Chapter Nineteen

Everyone was making their way into the great room jovial from playful dinnertime banter. They all seemed to be relaxed which is how Andre felt they should be before they were about to drop this difficult information upon them. Míchel was bringing the dogs in and situating them on their beds around the fireplace. He looked at Bernard and then his wife and began.

"May I have everyone's attention please?" He said in a business-like tone.

A palpable silence fell over the room. Evie noted that her father looked...what was it...nervous? He was antsy and hesitant. She had never seen him behave this way. He's cool and confident, not...anxious and unsure. Whatever he needed to tell the family definitely wasn't good news.

"I have some very important news to disclose regarding the events that have taken place and why we are all here." He paused. "Where do I start...?" He said to himself. Clearing his throat he began again.

"The man that attacked and tried to kidnap you this morning Evie was an assassin. He's a hired gun that usually works for anyone that is willing to pay his fee."

Evie went still, barely breathing.

Bernard put a hand on his brother's shoulder and took over. Andre stepped aside as Bernard took up the delivery of the facts.

"He is a man from my past." He looked at Bryce and Pierre. "You were right in your thinking that I was no ordinary Marine. I wasn't. I cannot disclose who or what I really am due to that information being highly classified. However, I can tell you that over the years during my illusive career, I have made many enemies." He was looking around the room at everyone's face to see their reactions. His eyes settled on Evie's face.

"Then..., during my last assignment as an operative in the field, I met your mother."

112

"My mother?" Evie said confused. She looked at Alexis who was beginning to cry silent earnest tears that were streaming down her face. She looked back at Bernard. "Oncle…I…I don't understand." She stammered. She looked at Andre and Alexis once more and asked, "Aren't you my…my mother…my father?" She asked looking from one to the other.

Before Alexis could answer her question, Bernard answered for her. "She is your Tante Missy. She is your aunt." He let that sink in for a moment. "I..." He hesitated. Then in a gentle resigned voice he said, "…I am your father."

Evie's eyes began to swim with tears. She felt light-headed. She couldn't believe what she was hearing. This all had to be some huge misunderstanding or a nightmare. She was dreaming. She had to be dreaming. Confusion was evident in her eyes and body language. Josie stood and moved to her side. She reached to hug her but Evie flinched and leaned away. Josephine shot her father an angry look. She looked him in the eye and said through clinched teeth, "Explain!"

"This isn't easy for me Chéri…" he started.

Josie cut him off. "I don't care Père! Explain!"

Bernard glanced around the room. The men had confused but speculative looks on their faces. The women, however, were confused and becoming angry.

"Let me start from the beginning…" He said in a quiet voice. "My name is Vincent Bernardo DeGaul." A collective gasp filled the room. "I am not Andre's long time family friend, I am his younger brother. We have the same father but different mothers. That is why we share the same last name. I was recruited by a covert government agency right out of boot camp, trained as a field operative and deployed overseas. I was very good at what I did and before I knew it I was working for multiple agencies in deep cover operations. This is why you never met your Uncle Vincent." He sighed and continued. "Your mother, Evie, was involved with another man when I met her. He was a dangerous man that we were investigating. We were infiltrating his operation to destroy it. Initially, we thought that she was part of his operations, but later learned that she was merely being used because of her father's connections."

Evie spoke. "None of this makes any sense to me." She looked at Alexis who was crying earnestly in Andre's arms now. "I have her eyes...?" She said questioningly. "How is it that I have her eyes if I am not her daughter?"

"Because, Evie..." he said in a gentle voice. "Your mother was her twin sister."

"This is madness!" Josie shouted. "How could you? How could you do this to her...to us? Josie looked to her father and then to her aunt and uncle. They were all focused on Evie.

Evie was staring at all of them blankly with unfocused eyes. She could not believe what she was hearing. She was trembling. Her entire body was shaking as if there were no fire in the massive fireplace and it had suddenly begun to snow right there in the room. After a long silence, she finally spoke. "What was my mother's name?" She looked up then to stare into his eyes. She saw sorrow, compassion and pain flash through them in succession.

In a hoarse voice he answered, "Her name was…was Geneviève Marie Cartier. You do have your mother's eyes, Evie, and her name. She was Alexis' identical twin sister. Let me explain further. I cannot tell you everything, but I will tell you what is important and what I can reveal." He glanced around the room once again before he spoke. "As I said before, I met your mother during my last operation, we fell in love and I decided to take a different…well what I thought to be a safer job than being an, in the field, operative. In short, I took a desk job, so to speak. I was offered an opportunity in the S.O.D. within the State Department.

By this time, Pierre and Bryce had both looked up and sat forward.

"Special… Operations… Division... I knew it." Bryce said out loud but more to himself. Vincent's confession confirmed his suspicions.

"Yes, that's right." Vincent answered him without looking away from Evie.

My partner was not happy about me leaving and warned me that things had a way of catching up to us, especially under the circumstances surrounding your mother and how we came to be together. But, my mind was set and I moved forward with my plans. Two years later, your mother was killed by the man we believe sent the assassin to kidnap you. She was killed by the very same man..." he paused. "...on the day you were born Evie." He caused your mother to run her car off the road and into an embankment. She survived long enough for them to save you."

"That's why you were crying when you brought Evie home maman? Pierre spoke in a quiet thoughtful voice. Understanding was dawning in his eyes. "That was the part I could never understand. I was so young... I didn't understand why you were so sad. Why everyone was so sad."

"Oui, I had just lost my sister...my twin. We were inseparable and then suddenly she was gone." Alexis acknowledged Pierre's statements.

Andre spoke next, "We were attempting to keep the family safe. If the man who killed your mother knew that the baby had survived he would have come after her too. And, we just couldn't bear that."

"So I hid you with my brother and his wife until I neutralized the threat. Vince continued. "I went after Horace Drakkar. The scar on his face was from my knife. I was unsuccessful in killing him but he bares my mark."

Bryce, who had remained silent during the meeting for the most part, was shaking his head in disbelief. "We have had run-ins with this man before...Pierre and I. We may have inadvertently blown your cover."

"It is possible. Like I said, the man we are dealing with has no master. There is no specific agency or group or individual that he works for solely. He is a contractor, a simple gun for hire. There is no job he will refuse if his fee is met. The man has no scruples."

Evie was trying to concentrate on what was being said. The words seemed to swirl all around her and she was having a hard time comprehending them. She silently counted to ten to focus before she began speaking.

"Let me see if I have this right…" She paused to gather her wits and took a deep calming breath. "My parents are my aunt and uncle and my uncle is my father? And, my mother is dead…? My brothers are my cousins and my cousins are my siblings?"

"Yes."

"And…and now…there is a madman after me because of you or because of who I am or because of my dead mother?" She paused, beginning to take short shallow breaths.

"Probably for all of those reasons Missy." Vincent answered.

"Okay…okay." She stood and in an eerily calm voice said, "I'm going to my rooms now. Thank you for the information…I think…?" She whistled for Serge and in a flash he was at his mistress's side.

No one made a move to stop her. There wasn't a person in the room who even knew what to say. The tension in the room was so thick it was palpable, as if you could simply reach out and almost touch it. She silently left the room without so much as a look backward or an offered word or question. Once she was out of earshot the room erupted. Josie was pissed and firing questions at her father while she sobbed. Lucy went to her side to attempt to comfort her daughter.

"How could you Père? How could you?" It was all she seemed to be able to say. She turned her angry eyes onto her mother who was also crying now. "Did you know maman? Did you?" She asked accusingly.

"No sweetheart. I didn't know. I was off at the university when our sister was killed. I only knew that she had been in a car accident. I didn't even know she was pregnant or that Geneviève belonged to her. I just assumed that your Tante named her after our sister because she was killed. Nor did I know that Bernard wasn't Bernard at all." She looked at her husband thoughtfully.

"No one but me, Andre and Alexis knew about the baby." Vincent explained. "We thought it best if no one knew in order to keep her safe. We told no one. We thought it best to simply change the family a bit to confuse any enemy that may have been searching for me, but we wanted to keep the family core together. So, we hid Geneviève in plain sight when she survived the accident that took her mother."

Lucy took her daughter's hand and squeezed it. Josie's initial shock and anger was beginning to subside. She allowed Lucy to comfort her.

Míchel and Rogét, who had remained utterly silent during the entire meeting, finally spoke. Míchel spoke first saying, "Well, now we know. What are we going to do about this very confusing situation?"

Rogét inquired, "Hold on…before you answer that question…" he said with his hands raised palms out. "…is there anything else you need to share. Might as well put it all on the table now is my thinking."

"Yeah…sure…drag out all the skeletons from that goddamned closet and beat us all over the head with them!" Míchel said sarcastically. "I'm positive my headache can't possibly get any worse."

"There is nothing more. That was and shall remain our family's deepest darkest secret. I don't think I need to say this but I will say it anyway…Evie's true identity needs to remain a secret to the outside world. No one, and I do mean no one, outside this room need ever know who she really is. I sincerely hope that each and every one of you understands the gravity of this situation and can keep this secret forever."

Everyone sat in silence for a moment. Vincent took a long breath and opened the floor for questions from the family and offered explanations as best he could. Then everyone, both physically and mentally exhausted, decided in unison to call it a night and turn in. One by one they left the great room and made their way to their respective suites until only Vincent and Andre remained.

"Well that went better than I expected." Vincent said on a sigh.

"Yeah...too well. I'm worried about Evie, Vince. She was too calm."

"She was in shock. I'd just told her that her parents were not her parents and...well you know the rest. Sounds like a bad soap opera!" Vincent said in disgust.

"We knew that this day would come brother. Don't beat yourself up. Trust me, when she regains her wits about her, she will do it for you." Andre consoled, placing a hand on his brother's shoulder.

"It's time for bed. Our wives need us Vincent. Go to bed and we'll deal with this more in the morning."

"You're right. I suppose this is truly enough for one day. I think we are all feeling overwhelmed."

They embraced in a one-armed man hug. "You did well baby brother. You did very well. They will all sleep on it and see the logic of our decision tomorrow. Good night Vince."

Vincent smiled at his brother. "Good night."

They turned to leave the great room and Vincent's cell phone rang. He stopped and answered his phone. Andre waited patiently for the few seconds it took for Vincent to listen to the call.

"We need to get to the situation room." Vincent said as he disconnected.

They made their way down the hall to the situation room. Vincent connected his cell phone to the telecommunication pad. Malcolm's face materialized on the middle big screen.

"I do not have good news my friend." Malcolm stated in a grave voice.

"Any news at this point would not be good Mal." Vincent replied.

Malcolm, seeing Andre standing next to Vincent, acknowledged his presence with a nod. "Andre."

"Malcolm. I would say it's nice to see you again but under the circumstances…"

"The feeling is mutual. This is a hairy situation." He turned his attention back to Vincent. "I know who's behind the attempted kidnapping of Evie, Vince."

"Who?"

"Alkis Georgiou! Remember him?"

"I knew it. Goddamn it! I knew it had to be him."

"The man you were investigating when you met Evie's mother?" Andre guessed.

"Yes." Vincent and Malcolm answered in unison.

"Intel says that he has hired Horace Drakkar to kidnap Evie and kill Pierre and Bryce." Malcolm continued. "There's more…he's there Vince."

"Here in the States?" Vincent said, squinting his eyes in thought.

Malcolm leaned forward in his seat. "There… in California, Vincent."

Stunned, Vincent placed both hands on the desktop in front of him. "Here?" He looked at Andre. "Mal, does intel say why he's here in California."

"Intel says he's here in the states to pick up a very important package."

"Evie." Andre said quietly.

"Intel also says that Drakkar has men stationed within a thirty to fifty mile range of everywhere Evie's plane landed. So, for obvious reasons, keep a low, very low profile. They are in Susanville my friend."

"We anticipated that Mal. We're dug in here and secure. They won't find us here. We're at the safe house that you helped build and design remember." Vincent said in a thoughtful voice.

"I do. However, I also know that Evie likes to disappear. Keep a close eye on her. If there is anything else you need. You know how to reach me."

"Thanks Mal. I'll be in touch."

They disconnected.

Andre and Vincent looked at each other.

"I don't like this Vince. It's too close to home."

"I don't either. There's nothing we can do about it tonight. We'll let everyone know in the morning."

"Agreed."

They both left the situation room with uneasy thoughts on their minds.

Chapter Twenty

It was late. Evie knew that everyone had gone to bed long ago. She'd escaped to her suite and let out all her emotions. Feeling as if her entire world was turned completely upside down, she'd cried until she had no more tears. No one had followed her and she was grateful for them allowing her privacy. She needed it at this moment and she didn't really want to face anyone right now. She was lying across her bed trying to come to terms with the fact that her life had been a lie. As the hours passed, she remained awake and lost in her own thoughts. She needed air. She needed out of this house.

She sprang out of bed seemingly renewed and on a mission. Serge's head popped up when she left her bed but he didn't move from his bed. She went to her closet and slipped on a pair of jeans and a t-shirt. Then, remembering that she was in the mountains and it was cold outside, added a soft warm sweater. She searched around for a pair of sneakers and put them on too. She donned a hat and matching scarf, grabbed a jacket and left the closet. She picked up her purse and signaled for Serge to follow her. "We'll just go for a short drive eh Serge? How about that...does that sound good to you?" She whispered to her four-legged companion as they moved silently through the house. They walked past the kitchen and into the great room. When she entered the foyer she opened the little box on the wall that held all the car keys. She spotted the keys to Míchel's new 2013 Range Rover. It boasted a

V8 5.0 liter engine, grained leather interior seats, a Meridian sound system and best of all, heated seats. "The perfect choice for my, just before dawn, foray." She said to herself. She punched in the code on the keypad by the front door to turn the alarm off and then repeated the code to turn it back on once she and Serge were out the door and had closed it behind them.

They were greeted by Beau, Sasha and Apollo as soon as they hit the driveway. She gave them each a scratch behind the ear and started towards Míchel's SUV with Serge on her heels. She pushed the button on the key fob that opened the rear hatch and Serge leaped in. She pushed the button again and the hatch closed. She got in and started the vehicle. The engine, surprisingly quiet, started without a hitch. She placed the gear in reverse and backed out of the parking space and then forward down the driveway to the unmarked road and onto the highway headed south. She drove into the little Township of Eagle Lake. Driving passed the little airstrip that her gulfstream had landed on the day before, she decided to continue on and turned right onto a road that would eventually lead to yet another road that would take her into Susanville. Evie didn't know where she was going. She was just driving. She needed air and space away from the family she thought she knew. She cracked the windows to let in the early morning fresh air. On the horizon, the sun was making its morning debut. It was slowly rising over the Sierra Mountains shooting off tiny fingerlike rays of light that danced on the lake in a shower of colorful sparkles. It would be light soon. The beauty and serenity of Eagle Lake was very calming and somewhat overwhelming. She felt caged and her emotions were roiling inside her mind. She needed to clear her head. So she kept driving.

She drove along the two-lane highway until she reached the sleepy town of Susanville. The darkness of the night sky was rapidly receding and the sun's warm and welcoming rays were filling the sky. On Main Street, she stopped at Starbuck's for hot tea and a slice of banana nut bread. There wasn't a drive-thru so she drove into the little parking lot and parked.

"I'll be right back." She said to Serge. She walked into the little café to stand in line to place her order.

Seated in the corner of the little seating area of the café, were the two men that Erik had staking out Susanville. One was seated facing the door and the other had his back to the door. When Geneviève drove up and stepped out of the car, the man facing the door recognized her immediately. He motioned to his companion to discreetly turn and verify that it was in fact her. His companion turned and did just that. They couldn't believe their luck. The man with his back to the door pulled out his cell phone and punched the number on speed-dial.

Horace Drakkar thought he heard a soft knock on his bedroom door. Awaking from a dead sleep he listened intently for the sound he thought he'd heard. Again, he heard the knocking. He looked at his clock on the nightstand next to the giant king-sized bed, 5:45am. This…had better be good. He got up and snatched up the robe that was lying carelessly across the little chair and put it on. He opened the door to find Erik standing on the other side.

"We've found her sir!"

"Where?"

"Susanville.   The men we have there spotted her at a Starbuck's in Susanville."

"Susanville?" Drakkar pondered. "The plane was a decoy. They got off at that little airstrip near Susanville. Excellent! Have them follow her only! Do not approach her." He commanded.

"Yes sir!"

"Erik…" he said calmly, "…wake the others. We will leave immediately and rendezvous with the men following her. Get us a private flight to Reno. We will drive from there."

"It will be done." Erik turned and went back to his suite to dress and wake the other two men.

Bryce's alarm went off at 8:00am. He'd decided to sleep in since everyone was gathered there in the same house. He stretched a long languid stretch and got out of bed heading for the shower. Fifteen minutes later, he was padding down the hallway towards Evie's bedroom door.   He didn't knock in case she was still sleeping. He tried the door…it was locked.

"Okay…" He said to himself. "She obviously doesn't want anyone disturbing her."

Respecting her need for privacy he turned and started towards the kitchen. He wasn't the only one awake he concluded. Míchel and Rogét nearly knocked him over when they both converged on the hallway at the same time headed towards the kitchen.

"Gentlemen…" He greeted them.

They both mumbled good morning and sleepily continued towards the kitchen.

"Coffee…" Rogét said in his best zombie voice. "I need coffee."

"There has to be some brewing Ro, I can smell it from here." Míchel said in a sleepy voice.

They stepped into the kitchen and searched out the coffee maker which was indeed brewing coffee.

"Bless the kitchen goddesses. They set the timer on the coffee pot. Bless them…oh bless them from the tops of their sweet heads to tips of their perfectly manicured little toes." Rogét chanted.

"You're sick man…you should seek professional help." Bryce chuckled.

"Hey! I'll have you know that my therapists say I am just fine!" He tossed back trying to keep a straight face.

"Therapists…?" Bryce stated flatly, a single eyebrow rising. "…As in more than one?"

"Didn't you know?" Míchel interjected as he poured himself a steaming cup of the fresh hot coffee. "Young Ro here has at least seven therapists, one for every single day of the week. He's…well…in a nutshell…certifiably insane."

"Hey! I resemble that remark!" They all laughed out loud and then shushed each other.

"Don't wanna wake the ladies before they get all their beauty rest. We'll never hear the end of it if we do." Bryce commented quietly.

"Too late!" Another sleepy voice announced from the kitchen doorway. "Step aside mere mortals, lest I slay thee for my morning mug of java." Josie said as she padded on socked feet into the room.

"M'Lady. Bryce gave her a graceful bow as he handed her the mug of coffee he'd just poured for himself. "I choose life so you may have my cup goddess. There will be no need for slaying this early in the morning."

"Ah hell, she doesn't count Bryce, she's just a sister." Rogét teased.

"Merci beaucoup, Monsieur. You are a well and faithful servant and I shall reward thee with wonderful home cooked meals." She smiled an appreciative smile then turned to glare at her brother. "You, however, will be lucky if you even get to smell it! It's air pudding and wind sauce for you knave!" She gave him a satisfied smug smile.

Míchel piped up then. "Ummm...goddess... I am on the side of my brother Bryce on this matter. You may have my mug of coffee, too, if it pleases thee."

"You may keep yours kind sir and you, too, shall be granted the pleasures of my culinary skills." Josie said graciously.

"Traitors!" Rogét feigned disgust. "I'm going out to feed and water the dogs. You two are pathetic."

"Nope, we're smart! She has us by the stomach man!" Bryce said laughing to Rogét's retreating back.

"Has Evie emerged from her rooms yet Bryce?" Josie asked him.

"I haven't seen her yet this morning Josie. I did stop by her door and it was still locked. I didn't knock because I figured she was still in privacy mode and when she's ready to come out and talk to us, she will."

"I was just curious." She said into her coffee mug as she sipped.

"I think I'm still in shock too." Míchel said. "It hit me hard. I can't imagine how it made her feel."

"She will need time. We all will. Our family bond is strong. We will get through this. I am sure of it." Josie said with confidence. "I think we just need to give her some space…"

"She's gone!" Rogét ran into the kitchen breathless. "She took my car! She and Serge are gone!"

All banter in the kitchen ceased.

"Are you sure?" Bryce asked. Already putting down the coffee mug and striding quickly towards Rogét. "Are you positive Ro?"

"Yes goddamn it! Evie and Serge are gone! I checked her room after I noticed my vehicle was missing. I unlocked the door to her rooms. They're gone!"

Pierre appeared in the kitchen doorway rubbing his eyes. "What's with all the ruckus?" He asked in a sleepy voice. "People are trying..." his voice faded away when he saw the look on everyone faces. "What?"

"Evie is gone Pierre." Bryce said, his expression turning grave.

"Shit! Sorry Josie."

"Shit is right! Don't apologize on my behalf. Not right now. What are we going to do Pierre?"

"Wake the other's. We need to start searching for her now."

Chapter Twenty-One

Evie had her tea and banana loaf and was headed back to the car. As she got in and settled, putting her tea in the cup holder and placing her loaf in her lap, she smiled at the two men that were also leaving the café as she replaced her seat belt. She didn't want to seem unfriendly but she didn't want to be talkative either. So she just smiled and continued on her way.

She put the car in reverse and backed out of the parking space. A few seconds later she was leaving the little parking lot and headed south towards the interstate.

Evie didn't have a certain destination in mind, she just wanted to drive. She figured she'd drive for an hour or so then turn around and retrace her steps to go back to the house. She knew everyone would be upset with her, but she didn't care. She was an adult. She could take care of herself. So she drove with the windows cracked and enjoyed the sunrise and the fresh mountain air.

Jan and Hector, the two men from the café, followed Evie as she drove onto Interstate 395 headed towards Reno. Jan was driving so he instructed Hector to make the phone call and update the boss on the current situation. Hector pulled out his cell phone and hit the number on speed dial.

"She is headed south on Interstate 395 towards Reno." He stated when the line on the other end was answered.

"Did you make any contact with her?" Erik asked.

"No sir. She did see us leaving the little café and smiled at us, but that is all. I do not believe she knows that we are following her. This highway is fairly straight and there are several cars between us. She is driving a silver 2013 Range Rover."

"Excellent. We will be in Reno in an hour. Once we land we will make our way north and close the distance. Then we will have her. Continue following her. Let me know if anything changes." He disconnected.

Erik relayed the information to Drakkar who was sitting next to him on the tiny private jet.

"Excellent! I will be able to deliver my package today. Our client is on his way to Los Angeles as we speak. Today is a good day Erik."

The DeGaul safe house was in full gear. Everyone was dressed and ready to go. Andre was watching Pierre break everyone into teams to search for Geneviève.

"Père I'm teaming up you and Oncle Bern…" He hesitated then quickly corrected himself. "Oncle Vincent."

"Míchel, you're with Rogét. Bryce you're with me. Ladies, I want you to search the little town here in Eagle Lake but I don't want you going any further than that. I don't want to risk anyone seeing you that shouldn't. I don't think anyone knows we're here, but you never know so be careful."

Pointing to the map of the area that he'd placed on the table so everyone could see it, Pierre pointed to each quadrant he'd circled and assigned a search team.

"We'll keep in contact with each other via our secured satellite cell phones. No one take any unnecessary risks. No one!" He glanced around the room at all the worried faces. "We will find her. We have to. I don't think she would have gone very far." His eyes settled on his father's. Andre inclined his head in a nod of approval.

"Let's waste no more time. Move out."

Everyone scattered.

"Josie!" Míchel shouted over his shoulder as he grabbed the keys to one of the vehicles. "I am taking Sasha with me.

Pierre is taking Beau. We are leaving Apollo for you. Use him if you need to. You know what to do."

"Got it. Yes I do." She answered over her own shoulder. "Go!"

"Gone!"

"I will stay behind in case she shows up back here." Alexis volunteered.

"That's a good idea Tante. I will leave Apollo with you so you are not alone. We won't need him in the car with us. We won't be leaving the vehicle during our search of the town. There are only two public places. If she isn't at either of the convenience stores, then our part of the search will be over and we will return here to the house." Josie said. "Call us if she returns."

"You know I will."

"We'll be back." Josie and Lucy hurried to their designated vehicle. The search for Geneviève was in full swing.

Pierre and Bryce slipped into their vehicle and sped off down the driveway and onto the unmarked road that led to the highway.

"It's my fault Pierre! I should have kept a vigil. I should have anticipated this." Bryce said in dark and intense voice.

"Don't even go there! We will find her." Pierre replied. "We have to so I can kill her myself!"

"We don't even know how much of a head start she has on us. But I'm betting it's at least two hours." Bryce contemplated.

"We will stay out here until we find her. My little sister…cousin…shit… whatever she is…she's damned smart. She will find her way home or we will find her."

"You're right of course. I'm just hoping we find her before anyone else does."

Evie had been driving for almost two hours. She was beginning to feel much more relaxed and the fog that was clouding her mind was beginning to clear. She didn't quite have a handle on all of the emotions she was feeling at the moment, but she wasn't feeling that sappy annoying need to cry anymore. For that, she was thankful. Evie hated to cry. But, thankfully, that part of this emotional rollercoaster she was riding was over. She was finally coming to terms with all she had learned the night before. She really did understand the logic of her parent's decision surrounding the events of her birth and her biological mother's death. Logically, it made perfect sense. She hadn't been stolen or anything drastic like that. They simply kept her true paternity a secret in order to keep her safe.

"Well hell…" She said to Serge who was lounging in the back seat. "They kept me safe Serge. They kept the family together." She chewed on her bottom lip. "I should be thankful and grateful, shouldn't I?"

Serge looked at his mistress and tilted his head a little. She smiled at him in the rearview mirror. He took that as an invitation and leaped into the front seat with one graceful bound. Evie reached over and scratched him behind the ears. Then she rolled down the window completely so he could stick his head out and enjoy the wind. He did just that. Stuck his head out the window with his tongue lolling and enjoyed the wind. Evie laughed.

"There's a rest stop a few miles down the road. I think we've driven far enough don't you?" She said to him. "We'll stop there and get you some water and let you stretch your legs and do your business, okay?"

Keeping his big head out the window, Serge wagged his big tail in response to Evie's voice.

Twenty minutes later they were pulling into the rest stop. Evie parked the SUV and got out. She let Serge out and he sat patiently by her side waiting for a command.

"Ladies first." She said. "I need to visit the little girl's room." They walked casually and unhurriedly towards the ladies facilities.

Evie did not notice the sleek black BMW that parked on the other side of the parking lot.

Jan and Hector watched Evie go into the ladies room.

"She has a dog with her." Hector said absently.

"I noticed that." Jan answered speculatively.

"Do you think it's a factor?" Hector wondered out loud.

"Depends, but I think not. Call the boss and give him an update."

Hector once again pulled out his cell phone and called Erik. Erik picked up on the first ring.

"We are at a rest area on I395 about an hour and a half south of Susanville. She has a dog with her. They are in the ladies restroom." He said into the phone.

"We are a half an hour away. We will meet you there." Erik disconnected.

Evie and Serge emerged from the restroom. She gave him a release signal and Serge took off for the grassy area. He happily watered all the surrounding shrubbery and sniffed everything and everyone he came into contact with. Evie sat on the park bench and watched him. He seemed to need a little freedom and fresh air too she mused.

The rest area wasn't very big. But it was well kept and boasted a nice little grassy area with two small benches, restrooms and a few vending machines with a nice variety of sodas, juices and snacks for anyone who wished to stop and stretch their legs or use the facilities.

She glanced around the area enjoying the sunshine that was warming the brisk morning air when she noticed the black BMW with two men inside it. She kept her eyes moving as if she hadn't seen them but a chill of unease crawled up her spine. She had seen those two men before. They were the men she'd smiled at when she was leaving the coffee shop. Their vehicle wasn't in the parking lot when she arrived. She thought to herself. Were they following her? Adopting a look of complete relaxation and casualness she whistled for Serge.

Smiling at him while holding back the bile of panic that was threatening to overtake her senses, she hugged him and scratched his ears.

"Are you ready to go Serge? Everyone should be up by now and we don't want them to worry." He licked her hands barking and whining in his usual excited way.

She stood and they began to casually make their way unhurriedly to the Range Rover. She didn't dare look over to where the men were parked again, but she knew they were watching her. She just kept smiling and talking to her canine companion as they made their way back to the vehicle.

She opened the driver's side door and let Serge in and followed in after him. Trying not to look as if she were escaping, she put her seatbelt on and started the engine. She backed out of the parking space and drove back towards the interstate's northbound entrance. She looked in her rearview mirror to see if the black BMW was following her and was just about to breathe a sigh of relief when she saw it, too, back out of the parking space it was occupying and make its way onto the northbound entrance.

"Damn it Serge, they are following me!" Serge looked at her and tilted his head slightly as if he were really trying to understand her.

Evie chewed on her bottom lip while she contemplated how to handle the situation.

"Well…merde, Serge!" She said when she spotted a second black BMW behind the one following her. She couldn't tell how many men were in that vehicle but she knew instinctively that they were there for her.

Evie thought about her options. She didn't have many. She was at least an hour and a half from the safe house. She could call Pierre and tell him… "Tell him what?" She thought to herself. "Tell him that I was stupid enough to leave the safety of a safe house? Oh yeah, that will go over like a fart in an elevator!"

She looked at her companion. "Don't worry. We will find a way out of this mess."

She glanced at her rearview mirror again. The two BMW's were four cars behind her. They didn't seem to be making any aggressive moves. They simply continued to follow her. Not wanting to compromise the location of the safe house, she rifled through her purse for her cell phone and called the only person she felt might not yell at her as much as she deserved.

Chapter Twenty-Two

Horace Drakkar and his entourage followed close behind Jan and Hector. They'd finally made it to the rest area as their quarry was leaving. She seemed to be completely unaware of their presence and Drakkar was confident that she would lead them back to the DeGaul's hidden lair.

"Erik, move in front of Jan. I want our vehicle in front."

Erik maneuvered their vehicle into the lead position nodding at Jan as they passed.

"She doesn't seem to be aware of our presence, Sir." Erik said.

"No she doesn't. This is a good thing. She may very well lead us back to her family's safe house. I know they have them all over the world. Makes sense that they would have one hidden deep in the mountains here in California." He answered in a contemplative voice.

"Do you think it wise to follow her home?" Erik cautiously inquired. He knew better than to question the actions or any decision of Drakkar.

"You may be right, Erik. I am sure that it would be under a heavy guard which we are unprepared for. We will have to take her before then and draw out Pierre DeGaul and Bryce Marten."

Erik nodded in agreement. Ian and Ivan were accompanying Drakkar and Erik riding silently in the back seat but listening intently to the conversation.

"We will wait for our opportunity to present itself. When we reach the seclusion of the mountain roads we will make our move." Drakkar said finally.

They continued to follow Evie keeping their distance as not to alert her of their presence.

Bryce's cell phone rang. He glanced at the caller ID and answered it immediately. "Where are you?" He said in a calm but annoyed voice.

"Don't be angry…please…not now…I'm in trouble Bryce." Evie answered.

"Evie!" He took a deep calming breath. "Sweetheart…where are you?" He said firmly.

"I'm on the I395 Bryce. But I'm not alone. I have two black BMW's following me."

"Is that Evie?" Pierre bellowed from the driver's seat.

"Yes, and she's picked up two tails."

"Goddamn it Evie! I told you not to pull one of your disappearing stunts!" He yelled.

"Drive Pierre. You're not helping." Bryce said covering the receiver of his phone. "Evie we will meet you when you get back into the mountains above Susanville. Just keep driving calmly. We're coming."

"Okay…okay. I'll just keep driving. I'm sorry Bryce." She said.

"Not now Evie. Later okay? Everything will be just fine. You'll see."

"Okay."

"Listen to me carefully Evie. I'm going to give you directions and instructions. Stay calm and we will get you back to us safely. Keep your cool. You're good at that."

"You're just trying to make me feel better Bryce Marten. Flattery will get you everywhere." She said on a shaky sigh. "I don't mind telling you that I am struggling to keep it together."

"You have to keep your head Evie. Serge is with you. I'm sure your pursuers have no idea of what he's capable of." Bryce reassured her. "Now listen carefully. Stay on the I395 to the 36 which will take you back into Susanville."

"Okay…" Evie was listening intently filing away every instruction that Bryce gave her in her mind.

"Stay on Main St, that's the 36. It will turn into Hillcrest Road. Do not make any turns. Got all that so far?"

"Yes."

"Before I go on, what is your location now?"

"I'm about 30 miles south of Susanville." She answered.

Bryce gave a low whistle. "How far did you drive Evie?"

"About an hour and a half south of Susanville Bryce…I know! I know! Before you read me the riot act…I know! And, I'm really sorry."

He sighed holding back his temper and frustration and giving Pierre the eye warning him to do the same.

"Don't worry about that now Evie. I'll be angry with you later when you're safe. Right now I'm simply trying to get you out of harm's way."

"Okay." She said on another sigh. "I know I've really messed up this time. But I will file that away for now and follow your instructions. I should be in Susanville in about twenty minutes or so. Traffic is very light."

"Good. That's great. Just keep going. Okay here is what you will do once you're on Hillcrest Road. Follow it to the County Highway A1 which is Eagle Lake Road. That's the name of the road you were on when you left this morning Evie. I'm simply taking you back the way you came. Okay?"

"Okay. I remember the route I took to go into town there in Susanville."

"Good. Then just go back the way you came. When you reach Baja Way, turn right onto it. Baja Way will fork Evie, so stay to the left. Go about a mile past the fork and park on the side of the road and let Serge out. Pretend you are letting him out to do his business. Head for the trees and don't look back. We will be there ahead of you but you will not see our vehicles or us. But don't panic, I promise you we will be there."

"Okay Bryce. I think I'm at least forty-five minutes from there though." She said her voice steady now.

"That's plenty of time for us to get there ahead of you, Evie. We'll be there. See you there." He reassured her.

"Okay. See you there." They disconnected.

Bryce was dialing and talking to Pierre at the same time. Pierre was fuming and attempting to rein in his temper. "Damn it! Damn it! She never listens to me. Why doesn't she ever listen to me?"

"Doesn't matter now, she needs us and we're going make things right and safe for her. Actually, we may have an opportunity to make everyone safe again. Míchel!..." he said into his phone.

"Yeah…did you find her?

"Yes and no! No time to explain, just listen!" Bryce gave Míchel the situation and told him the plan."

"Do we have time to make it there? We are on the south end of the lake near the Eagle campgrounds." Míchel said. "It will take us at least a half an hour to get to that location."

"Get there faster. Make it twenty minutes Míchel. We will meet you and Rogét there."

"You sure this will work?" Míchel asked.

"We have our weapons and the dogs. I think we have the advantage." Bryce said with major confidence." He disconnected and began dialing again.

"We are about fifteen minutes from there." Pierre noted.

"Yes, I'm calling your father and see if they are within that time frame too. We may need all the help we can get."

Chapter Twenty-Three

Forty minutes later, Evie was turning onto Baja Way. She kept to the left when the road split. Drove a mile in and parked on the side of the road. She didn't see the 2 black BMW's but she knew they weren't far behind her.

Just as she was closing her car door she spotted them out of the corner of her eye. They were just around the bend. They stopped and parked as well. She pretended not to pay any attention to them as she leisurely opened the passenger's side door to let Serge out. Then they headed for the trees.

Drakkar and his men stopped when Evie stopped.

"What is she doing?" Erik said out loud.

"It looks like she is letting the dog out to do its business." Hector said from the back seat.

"I told you an opportunity would present its self." Drakkar commented with a malicious grin. "Go and retrieve her. Unharmed." He commanded.

"And the dog?" Ian inquired as he got out of the car.

"Leave it or shoot it. I don't care. Just get me the girl."

"It will be done." Ivan nodded.

Ian and Ivan were out of the vehicle and walking with Hector and Jan towards the tree line that Evie had entered.

Having arrived fifteen minutes before Evie, Bruce, Pierre, Míchel and Rogét were situated around a tiny clearing in the midst of the trees. They saw Evie drive up and park. They also noted the two black BMW's that followed close behind her. Bryce gave the signal and everyone fell back deeper into the thick trees concealing themselves in the shadows. Míchel had Sasha at his side and Pierre was handling Beau.

Bryce was watching them through a pair of tiny binoculars. He turned to his party and relayed the information in a whisper. "Six men total, four following Evie and two staying behind. Fan out and flank them." They all cautiously and silently moved into their positions and waited.

Evie didn't see any sign of her brothers or Bryce, but she knew they were there. Serge was on alert and he was beginning to whine. He was telling her exactly where each man was positioned when he whined and sniffed the air in all directions.

"I know they are here, Serge. Be patient. If I know my brothers, I know they have a plan." She assured him in a barely audible voice. Evie knew she was being followed. The men behind her made no effort to conceal their footsteps. Serge turned and began to growl menacingly. Geneviève turned in time to see four men enter the clearing. She sucked in her breath when she recognized the two men from the café that morning.

"Mademoiselle if you would please follow us." The tall blonde man said. His accent was thick.

Serge began to bark. She ordered him to stay by her side. He did but continued to bark his warning to the man directly in front of her. He was pointing a gun at her and he was wearing a smile on his face that did not reach his cold calculating blue eyes.

"Who are you? What do you want with me?" Evie demanded. She spotted movement behind the men but kept up her air of defiance.

"Mademoiselle…" The man said taking a step toward her. "Please do not make this difficult. Come quietly or I will have to shoot your companion."

Evie gave Serge the hand signal for silence. It was an almost imperceptible movement of her hand that he saw and obeyed immediately. Then she gave him the command signal for watch and wait. She knew that he would strike the moment the man got too close to her. She also knew that the other men were being flanked by her family and the other dogs. Sasha and Beau were in already in position watching and waiting.

Evie heard movement behind her. The man with the gun hesitated as he saw a man materialize from the shadows of the surrounding trees.

"I believe the lady would rather not go with you." Bryce told him. "Hello Hector. Long time no see. I see you're still working for the lowest scum of the earth."

"Monsieur Marten. What a nice surprise. Since you are to be disposed of as well, this will make my boss very happy. It is so nice of you to join us. You will put down your weapon now or I will shoot Mademoiselle here and her damned dog."

"I am unarmed. I have no weapon on me."

Evie couldn't believe what she was hearing but she kept silent. Did he really show up unarmed? Bryce began to raise his arms very slowly. Beau and Sasha burst from their hiding places and took down Ivan and Ian who were flanking Hector and Jan. Pierre and Míchel were shouting commands and taking down Jan in the ensuing chaos. Hector made a grab for Evie's arm holding the gun on Bryce.

"I will kill…" His words were cut off and replaced with screams of agony as Serge attached himself to Hector's groin. Hector shot wildly before Beau and Sasha each latched onto an arm. The gun went flying out of his hand as he hit the ground hard.

Bryce tackled Evie to the ground shielding her body with his from the bullets whizzing past them. Rogét called off the dogs and turned Hector's bleeding body over to secure his hands with a zip tie. Pierre and Míchel secured Ian and Ivan in the same fashion and each man was face down in the dirt.

"Evie are you hurt?" Bryce checked her body for bullet wounds.

"I'm fine and you're squashing me!" She said breathlessly.

"Pierre!" Bryce jerked his head towards the street not moving from his position shielding Geneviève. "Drakkar!"

Pierre, Míchel and Rogét took off in a dead run towards the parked cars leaving the dogs to stand guard over the bodies of the captured men. As they broke through the tree line they saw one of the BMW's leaving the scene. Pierre cursed creatively.

"Yep. That about sums it up!" Míchel said angrily.

"No way we can catch them Pierre." Rogét said stating the obvious. "Our cars are too far away and they will be long gone by the time we get this scene cleared."

"Yes, I know." Pierre said disgusted. "Let's get back to the clearing. Maybe we can get some information out of his henchmen!"

Evie struggled to breath underneath Bryce's heavy body but she did not try to move him. Sensing her struggle, Bryce shifted his weight and slid off to her side still checking her over for injury.

"You're bleeding!" She said. "You've been shot not me! Get off Bryce. Let me look at it."

"It's just a flesh wound Evie, a through and through. It's nothing. Are you sure you're not hit." He asked her again.

"YES! I'm sure." She said exasperated. "Now get off of me, please. So I can breathe again!"

He stood and helped her to her feet. She stood and swayed a little. He steadied her.

"I'm fine. Stop hovering." She said dusting the leaves and debris from her clothes. "It's just the adrenaline rush subsiding. Let me have a look at your arm."

"Not now Evie. It's fine. We have to get you out of here."

She turned to walk away from him and he gently grabbed her wrist effectively turning her around to face him.

"Bryce I said I was..." Her words died off when she saw the look he was giving her. She had tears in her eyes that she was desperately trying to keep from spilling over her lids.

"Geneviève...please." He said gently.

"I'm sorry." She said quietly. "I'm so sorry Bryce. I just wanted, no needed, some space. I really wasn't trying to be defiant. There's so much going on!"

He pulled her into his arms and let her cry. "It's okay. You're safe now." He put a finger under her chin and lifted her face to look into her beautiful teary grey-green eyes and pulled her closer holding her possessively. His lips were a breath away from hers. He thumbed an errant tear that was sliding down her cheek.

Movement in the trees caught his attention and broke the spell that seemed to envelop them. He looked up to see Pierre and the others returning. Bryce released Evie and turned to face the returning men.

"Did you get him? Wait, don't answer that. Obviously, you didn't because you're frowning."

"We didn't." Míchel answered irritated.

"The bastard got away. Erik Metzger was with him." Pierre said kicking dirt into Ian's face in frustration. Ian started to protest when he realized that there was a very big dog standing over him. Beau was poised to attack again giving his quarry a low warning growl.

"Oh please! Please! Make my day! I won't call him off this time." Pierre said in a voice dripping with sarcastic encouragement. He looked at Bryce. "Get her out of here. We will clean this mess up."

"Okay. Let's go Evie." He began to steer her out of the clearing towards the road. She turned to face her Pierre. She opened her mouth to speak then closed it when he looked at her. There was pain in his eyes and relief.

"Not now Evie. We'll talk about it later." He said gently.

"Oui. We will. I'm sorry Pierre." She spoke the words quietly then turned and allowed Bryce to lead her away. When they got back to the road, Andre, Vincent and someone else were waiting.

"Père!..." Evie started towards Andre then, realizing her mistake, she came to an abrupt halt. Confusion was evident all over her face. She looked from Andre to Vincent. Then she turned her attention to the other man standing with them. But before she could ask him who he was, Bryce stepped forward and placed a protective arm around her waist.

"Gentlemen." He nodded in acknowledgment. "I was just taking Evie home."

"Good idea." The other man said when Andre and Vincent remained silent, both men seemed to be locked in place by Geneviève's confused gaze.

"Pierre and the others are straight ahead. Drakkar's men are under control." Bryce told them.

"Thanks. We'll take it from here." Vincent finally spoke tearing his gaze away from Evie's to look at Bryce. "Please…take Missy home. And, Bryce…" He shook his hand. "Thank you…! You've been shot!" Vincent said abruptly.

"Anything for you Oncle… Oh, it's nothing… Really…just a simple through and through. Hurts like hell though.

I'll have it looked at when I get Evie back to the house." Bryce said.

He took Geneviève by the hand and led her back to Míchel's Range Rover. He opened the passenger's seat door and let her in. He closed her door and began to make his way around to the driver's side door.

The man that had arrived with Andre and Vincent was circling the car with a black rectangular shaped device in his hand. "I'm checking for any bugs or tracking devices that may have been applied while you were busy in the woods. As he made his way to the rear of the vehicle the little device he was holding beeped and all the lights began to flash red. He followed the beeps and located another device behind the license plate. He removed it and smashed it on the ground. He continued his search but didn't find any more unwanted tracking devices. He winked at Bryce and rejoined Andre and Vincent.

Bryce slipped into the driver's seat and put his seat belt on. Without a word, he started the engine, made a U-turn and started for home.

Geneviève was silent all the way back. When they turned onto the unmarked road that led to the house she spoke.

"I'm sorry Bryce. I just needed some space."

"It's ok, Evie. No one will hold your feet to the fire on this one."

"But…"

"Evie?" He said on a sigh. "What we were all told last night left us all a little shocked and angry. We all understand and share your frustration, anger and confusion. I just don't understand why you left the premises knowing that you were a target." Bryce parked the vehicle in the driveway and turned to look at her. "What the hell were you thinking?" He demanded.

"I wasn't thinking OKAY!" She threw her hands into the air in a gesture of complete frustration. "I just needed to get away!" She flung the car door open and slammed it shut but before she reached the stairs, Bryce caught her by the arm and swung her around.

"Damn it Evie! I thought I'd lost you!" The words were out of his mouth before he'd had time to think about what he was saying and censor his emotions.

"What?" She replied stupefied. "What did you just say?" Evie saw a mix of emotions flash across his face. There was concern, anger and something else.

"I…Evie I…"

"Oh my God! Geneviève Papillion DeGaul!" Alexis said sternly as she made her way down the front steps.

Evie turned to face her. "Mama"

"What were you thinking Chéri?" She stood in front of Evie and just looked at her. "Are you hurt?

"No maman."

"You're filthy, Chéri! What happened to you? No, nevermind, you can tell me later!" She ushered Evie up the remaining steps where Josie and Lucy were waiting. "Take Missy to her rooms Lucy please. I'll be there momentarily. Josie will you please get some food started? We will be in there to help as soon as we get Missy cleaned up and settled."

"Sure thing Tante!" Josie winked at Evie. "I'm so happy you're all right."

"Me too."

"Enough chit chat girls." Lucy said abruptly. "Let's get you cleaned up before we all dissolve into pitiful puddles of tears."

"I'll be there momentarily Luc. I need a word with Bryce." Alexis stood in the doorway waiting for him.

Bryce deflected the barrage of questions that Alexis had for him by simply saying, "You don't want to know, Tante Lex. Trust me, you'll sleep better not knowing how close we came to losing her."

Alexis hugged him. "You've been hurt! You're bleeding Bryce!"

"Nothing a few stitches can't fix Tante. I was hoping you'd help?"

"Yes of course!" Alexis said briskly. Let's go get you cleaned up too, Bryce."

"Thank you Tante." He kissed her cheek and headed for the First-aid room.

Chapter Twenty-Four

Horace Drakkar was furious. They had been totally unprepared for the opposition they met in that clearing. The DeGaul's were using dogs. As if, the men themselves weren't formidable enough. But goddamned dogs too! It was just infuriating. Once again, they had had the upper hand and he was damned tired of it. Right now, though, they needed to leave the area and possibly even the state to avoid being picked up by local authorities.

"Stick to the speed limit, Erik. We don't want any unnecessary attention." He ordered.

"Yes Sir. Are we heading back to the airport in Reno?"

"No. They will be looking for us there. Drive us to Los Angeles. I need to have a face to face with our employer." He pulled out his cell phone to hit the speed dial number for Alkis Georgiou but before he could press the button there was a loud bang and Erik lost control of the car. It flipped over several times and came to rest upside down on the side of the highway. He was only conscious long enough to see several black SUV's surround their overturned vehicle.

Pierre found Bryce pacing a hole in the great room's carpet in front of the fireplace.

"What? What is it? What's wrong Bryce?"

"Nothing…Everything!" Bryce threw up his hands in defeat and frustration.

"Evie isn't missing again is she? Pierre asked exasperated.

"No…no, nothing like that. Just nervous energy I suppose." He said on a sigh and stopped pacing.

"You're wearing a hole in the carpet. What's bothering you? And for God's sake, sit down! You're making me dizzy with all this panther-like pacing! I see my mother patched you up." Pierre said noting the bandaging across Bryce's shoulder.

Bryce sat in the overstuffed leather club chair across from Pierre. "Yes…she did." Bryce was silent for a long moment then he began talking almost to himself as if he were thinking out loud. "Things are just not adding up." Bryce said calming now. "We still don't know who is after Evie or why."

"I think…" Pierre hesitated when he heard the front door open and saw the three men enter the foyer in conversation. "I think we are about to find out." Both men got to their feet as Andre, Vincent and the man that had accompanied them at the scene entered the great room.

"Pierre, I would like you both in the situation room immediately." Andre said.

"Yes sir. We're right behind you. Lead the way." Pierre replied.

They all make their way down the hallways in silence. Míchel and Rogét were already in the room seated at the large oval shaped black granite conference table discussing the morning's events when they arrived. They stood when the men entered the room.

"Sit." Andre said. "We have a lot to discuss?"

"Beginning with introductions..." The mysterious man that had not been introduced as of yet began speaking. He was tall about six feet four inches, broad shouldered and had a thick mane of dark brown curly hair. "My name is Malcolm Divine."

"You are Vincent's ex-partner." Pierre stated understanding the connection between the two men now.

"Yes I am, although, our partnership was never truly dissolved. But that is a conversation for another day." Malcolm answered with a smile. "I was very proud to see that Vincent has trained you well. You performed and executed Evie's search and rescue like professionals."

"But the bastard we were after got away!" Bryce said.

"Well...not exactly. I did not come alone and my team caught up to Drakkar on Interstate 395. He had an unfortunate accident and we collected him and Erik Metzger at the scene." Malcolm explained. "They were both escorted to the local hospital for their injuries and are being detained there. They will be processed as soon as the doctor releases them."

"Ah, well that's great news. I hope you're planning to put that son of bitch in a cell somewhere truly horrific." Michel supplied with an evil grin rubbing his hands together.

"Do we know who he was working for?" Bryce inquired.

Vincent answered this time saying, "Mal's intel says it's a man named Alkis Georgiou. He is the man we were investigating and infiltrating when I met Evie's mother. She was seeing him and

I helped her see what a bastard he was. I think he may be holding a grudge." Vincent said with sarcastic humor.

Rogét blew out a long low whistle. "Ya think! Talk about motivation." He said. "That man held onto that grudge regarding Evie's mother for over two decades!"

Malcolm took over and said. "He won't be a problem anymore. He was intercepted at LAX before he could board his private jet and disposed of. There was a shoot out when my people tried to arrest him and he met an unfortunate end." Malcolm smiled. "He will not bother you again. However, I cannot stress the importance of keeping Evie's true paternity strictly in the family. Your uncle Vince here has a plethora of enemies. All of which would love to hurt him personally or through one of you." Malcolm stood silent for a moment contemplating his next statement carefully. "Although…after today's display of force and skill, I doubt anyone will be able to get near her again or any of you for that matter." He smiled again and looked directly at Bryce.

"What?" Bryce said a little embarrassed. "Am I that damned transparent?"

"Yes!" Everyone said in unison then they all laughed.

Chapter Twenty-Five

In the kitchen, Josie was busy whipping up some of Geneviève's favorite dishes and desserts. Lucy was acting as her soux chef and Alexis was tending to Evie's needs. Josie was attempting to keep herself busy trying to ward off fits of tears. It wasn't working. Lucy watched her daughter work and fight through her emotions.

"Why won't you let it go, Josie? Why won't you allow your emotions to flow? It's not healthy to keep it all in Chéri."

"Maman…I'm ok, really. I'm just a little overwhelmed. I thought we'd lost her. I thought I'd lost my cousin…no no wait…my sister and my best friend." She did let the tears flow now. She couldn't hold them back any longer. Lucy took a couple of steps to her daughter and embraced her. They shared a good cry and parted.

"She's home now Chéri. She's safe now."

"I know. And, she will be hard pressed to get away again. I don't think Bryce will ever let her out of his sight again." Josie returned wiping the tears away with a tissue. They both laughed.

Alexis entered the kitchen and took in the scene. "You two crying without me?" she teased.

"Sorry, couldn't help ourselves." Lucy said between sniffles. "Josie started it!"

"Maman!" Josie said laughing. "Did you just throw me under the bus?"

"Moi Chéri? Never! Just telling the truth is all." Lucy said feigning shock.

They all laughed again.

Alexis washed her hands and dove into the cooking. "Everyone is bound to have a hearty appetite after this morning's events."

"Oh oui!" Lucy exclaimed. "They will be foaming at the mouth soon."

"Let's get cookin' ladies!" Josie said smiling. "We've got our own private army to feed."

Geneviève sat on the gorgeous tiny antique settee in her closet dressing room applying her vanilla scented lotion. The little settee was upholstered with a beautiful blood red velvet material and had been hand carved from dark cherry wood. It was absolutely one of her favorite possessions that Bryce had so thoughtfully added to her quarters. She was finally alone and she contemplated the morning's events.

"That was really smart Evie." She said to herself. "Next time why don't you simply wrap yourself in a big red bow and deliver yourself to the bad guy personally!" She was scolding herself now. Past the point of tears now and anger was making its way through her emotional cycle. Alexis hadn't scolded or yelled or anything which only made her feel guiltier. She'd been nothing but supportive and she loved her for that. She reassured her that no one was angry with her and that they all understood her actions.

Albeit they were dangerous actions, but they understood and would not hold it against her.

"We're just glad that you are home safe now Chéri." Was all Alexis had said to her. Geneviève had apologized profusely, but Alexis wouldn't hear of it. She just kept saying she understood as silent tears streamed down their faces.

She'd settled Evie into her rooms and comforted her until she stopped crying and then left her alone because she knew her daughter would need her privacy.

"Take a bath Evie. It will make you feel better. I'll be in the kitchen helping to prepare lunch. Come and join us if you feel up to it." Then she'd quietly left the room.

Now, Evie sat alone in her dressing closet. She sat on her beautiful little settee contemplating her stupidity. She slipped into a pair of jeans and pulled on a sweater in her favorite color, pink. She grabbed a pair of slippers and socks for her cold feet and left the dressing room. She stopped short when she saw Bryce standing in the doorway of her room.

"I knocked...you didn't answer so I tried the door and it wasn't locked so I came in. I was just about to call your name when you came out of the bathroom. I'm sorry if I startled you."

"You didn't."

"Good. That's great." He said smiling nervously.

"I see you've been all patched up."

"Yeah, your mother has magic hands. She's a true healer, that woman."

"Oui, she is."

"I...I wanted to check on you...see how you were holding up."

"I'm fine. No worse for the wear you could say."

Evie was standing in the doorway of her bathroom. Bryce closed the distance between them in just a few strides and took her into his arms. The move was so abrupt that Geneviève had no time to react. He kissed her...hard. Greedily tasting her sweetness without giving her time to react or protest.

Geneviève's senses were reeling. One minute Bryce was in her doorway, the next she was in his tight embrace having her brain melted by the most passionate and unrestrained kiss she'd ever experienced. Her reaction was primal. She heard a small moan escape from within herself. His warmth and passion were overwhelmingly clouding her senses and she was drowning in it. He kissed her fiercely, deeply...possessively and she kissed him back with a passion that equaled his own. Then, just as abruptly, he released her.

"Apparently, you are the only person around here who doesn't know how I feel about you." He said, breathless. His dark expressive eyes were intense as they stared back at her. "Now you know!" He finished. Then, Bryce turned and stalked out of her room.

She stood there...blinking profusely. Her mind was struggling to reboot after the assault to her senses. Did she miss something? She thought desperately. What the hell was going on? What the hell had just happened?

Feeling a bit dazed and off balance she wandered down the hallway towards the kitchen. She could still taste his desire on her kiss swollen lips. Her body was humming and seemed to be on fire. His passion had awakened hers and she was, momentarily, at a loss for words.

The ladies in the kitchen were putting the finishing touches on lunch when Geneviève entered the room. Josie took one look at her and knew something was wrong.

"Oh honey…what's wrong?" She dropped the knife she had been slicing tomatoes with and went to Evie's side.

"Wrong?" Evie replied slowly.

"Chéri?" Lucy said concerned.

"Tell us Evie…" Alexis encouraged.

Evie looked at the three concerned faces standing in front of her. "Nothing is wrong…he…Bryce…"

"What Evie? Spit it out already!" Josie demanded.

"Bryce kissed me." Evie said finally.

It was silent in the kitchen for a split second then Josie shouted, "Well halleluiah! It's about time!"

"Is that what this is about?" Alexis asked gently. "He kissed you?

"Well…YES! It wasn't just any old kiss mama. When I stepped out of my bathroom, he was standing in my door way. He made a few attempts at small talk…asking how I was doing…you know…things like that. And, then, the next thing I knew my mouth was being assaulted and my knees were shaking!" Evie said puzzled.

Alexis cleared her throat trying to keep a straight face. "He didn't hurt you did he?"

"No! No…nothing like that. It was just….I don't know…so unexpected."

"Oh it wouldn't be." Lucy added stifling a laugh.

They were all smiling at her. Not only was she dazed but now she was confused.

"Okay…that's it! What is going on? How is it that everyone knows but me?" Evie asked exasperated.

"Ah well that's easy." Josie said mildly as she went back to slicing tomatoes. "You're retarded!"

"Josephine Amalie Cartier!" Lucy said in a reproving tone attempting, but failing miserably, to hide a smile and her laughter. "Evie is not retarded." She has simply failed to pay attention to body language. And…" Lucy threw up her hands to ward off Josie's comments. "And, now, I'm guessing that Bryce wanted to make his feelings painstakingly obvious." Lucy patted Evie's hand. "It's ok. Now you know."

Evie started laughing. It started out as a little confused giggle and ended up being a full belly laugh. They were all laughing. Tears were springing from their eyes.

Pierre cautiously entered the kitchen. "Ooooookaaay…" He said dragging the word out. "Ummmm….is this a bad time?

What's so funny? Should I be worried about the food you three are preparing?" he inquired with one dark eyebrow raised.

"Nope…" Josie said trying to straighten herself up again. "Your friend decided it was time to let Evie know how he felt."

"It's about time! What did he say to you Evie?"

"He didn't *say* anything! That's what made it so funny." Josie said, falling into another fit of laughter.

Beginning to chuckle himself because the laughter was contagious he asked, "Well then how *did* he tell her?"

"He kissed me…and I have to say…I actually agree with Josie aunt Luc. I am indeed retarded."

"He kissed you? HA! So much for subtlety!" He said, enjoying a good laugh himself. "Obviously, he's a man of few words."

"I think he's been trying to tell me all along and I just didn't see it. I had no idea."

"Well I hate to break the news to you le petit, but we all knew. And, you…well you've had a crush on him since you were in high school." Pierre reminded her.

"Oh you shush!" She punched him lightly in the arm. "That was supposed to be a secret blabber mouth."

"Not a secret Cheri." Alexis said smiling. "A mother knows when her daughter has a crush. You've been mooning over him for years."

The rest of the family and Malcolm piled into the kitchen with smiles on their faces drawn by all the unrestrained laughter wafting down the hallway.

"What's going on in here?" Andre's voice boomed.

"All is right with the world." Alexis answered him as he pulled her into his arms.

Bryce was the last to enter the big kitchen. When he spotted Evie, he stopped short and surveyed all the eyes looking at him. The family parted allowing him to walk directly to her. He strode confidently towards her smiling.

Evie, flushing with embarrassment and anticipation, stood where she was watching him approach her.

"Hi." He said watching her wary eyes.

"Hello." She answered him in a soft voice.

"You ok?"

"Oui, I think I'll survive."

"I…I want to apologize for…"

"Kissing me and walking away?" Geneviève finished for him. She placed her hands on her hips and raised one delicate eyebrow.

Bryce glanced around the room at all the expectant faces. Evie ignored them and concentrated on the man standing in front of her.

"Yes, something like that."

"What, exactly, are you apologizing for? Kissing me or walking away?" She inquired changing her stance from hands on hips to crossed arms over her chest.

Bryce paused for a moment, every bit aware that the entire room was watching the exchange.

"Well..." He began slowly. "I suppose I am apologizing for walking away. I will never apologize for kissing you. I love you Geneviève Papillion DeGaul." He took a step closer to her.

Evie attempted to take a step back and realized that she was standing in front of the kitchen island. There was no place for her to go so she stood her ground. She refused to look at all the faces looking at them for fear she'd melt into a puddle of embarrassment. Those were not the words she was expecting to hear. Actually, she didn't know what she was expecting, but it wasn't that. She stood her ground and watched him. Then, she thought to herself..."Oh my God! He's going to kiss me again. This time in front of everyone..."

Bryce, reading her thoughts, reached out for her and wrapped her gently in his arms before she could escape.

They were both smiling. Evie was dying from embarrassment and Bryce was loving every minute of it. She squirmed, just a little, to feign protest but he didn't let her go.

"I'm going to kiss you now Evie." He said in a low whisper. Then he lowered his head and kissed her.

Geneviève forgot her momentary embarrassment and held on to him kissing him back. Bryce knew better than to kiss her like he did in the bedroom with an audience, but he did put his feelings into it.

Hoots and hollers erupted all around them. Bryce gave her a couple of extra pecks and reluctantly released her. Josie pulled her away and hugged her. Pierre shook Bryce's hand and said, "It's about damn time!"

Vincent strode over to them both followed by Andre and Alexis.

"We give you our permission to date our Papillion." Andre said.

Bryce looked at Vincent.

Vincent simply nodded and with a crooked grin said, "It was all in the plan, son. I told you. It was all in the plan."

"What plan?" Bryce and Evie asked in unison.

The room erupted in laughter.

Epilogue

"Bryce and Evie should be here any minute." Pierre said.

"Good. They need to be aware of the situation." Malcolm stated flatly. He was angry. Everyone in the room was angry but determined.

"Do we know how many casualties the hospital sustained?" Vincent asked.

"A lot." Malcolm replied.

Pierre cursed.

Bryce and Evie entered the room. Bryce surveyed the room and noted the tension and unhappy faces.

"Something is wrong." Evie said, feeling a sudden sense of foreboding. "What's wrong?"

They were all sitting around the huge fireplace of the great room. Malcolm and Vincent the only ones standing. Malcolm spoke first.

"Horace Drakkar and Erik Metzger escaped custody this morning. They had a team rescue them and our men were outnumbered and out gunned."

Bryce pulled Evie closer to him.

"They killed several of the hospital's personnel and injured some of Mal's men as well in the melee." Vincent added, picking up the dialog. "They have been gone long enough now for us to assume they are headed out of the country. However, we all know what assumption does and we want all of you to be on high alert."

Malcolm looked at Pierre and Bryce. "The two of you are his main targets. So, you must remain vigilant. Close a net around Geneviève. He will most likely use her to get to you."

Malcolm looked directly into Geneviève's grey-green eyes and spoke softly. "Evie...I trust you will give Bryce and your brother your full cooperation."

"If you mean will I stay put and not pull one of my disappearing acts, then yes. I have learned my lesson. I will not go anywhere unescorted by either of them or the dogs."

The entire room breathed a sigh of relief. Then they all laughed releasing all of the pinned up tension in the room.

"Well that's half the battle won!" Míchel said teasing her.

"Oh shush you!" Josie said coming to Evie's defense. "It's not like you're a pillar of cooperation all the time."

"All right, all right…! Enough! Quiet down!" Andre said as he stood up and brought the entire room to attention, interrupting the chatter that was about to take over the room. "Let them finish briefing us so we can eat!" The room fell silent again.

Malcolm continued. "With your permission Evie, Vincent will continue to live with you on the island as your servant." He waited for her to agree.

Vincent stiffened, ready to be rejected.

Evie stood and crossed the distance between her and her father. When she reached him she paused for a moment to look into his eyes.

"I have had time to think about the actions and decisions that all of you made on my behalf as an infant."

"Missy…"

"Don't interrupt, it's rude remember?" She said, then she smiled at him.

Vincent relaxed a little and smiled back at her. "My apologies Missy."

"It is my belief that all of you made those decisions to keep our family safe from harm, to keep *me* safe from harm. I always knew that there was something special between us. I just didn't know what it was. Now I do."

She looked at Andre and Alexis. "You will always be my parents. You will always be my mother." Evie said, looking at the only mother she knew. Alexis had tears in her eyes.

"Don't cry!" She said laughing. "You'll make me cry, too!"

"They are happy tears Chéri." Alexis said, swiping her tears with her delicate hands.

Evie looked around the room. Lucy and Josie were crying too. "Damn it." She said laughing as the tears began to streak down her cheeks as well. "You know crying is contagious!" She returned her gaze to Vincent and said, "Don't you dare!"

He chuckled and pulled her into a tight hug. "I wouldn't dream of it Missy. Men don't cry."

"I do have one request." She said, pulling away from his embrace.

"Just one?" He teased.

"Oui, just one." She said smiling at her father.

"Ok…what would you like?"

"I would like for you to call me by the name that you gave me…" She said tentatively.

Pain shot through him momentarily rendering him speechless. Recovering quickly he said, "I loved your mother fiercely Missy. I want you to know that. When she was taken from me and you were all I had left, I gave you her name. It was the highest honor in my mind that suited you both. However, I had a hard time saying the name without feeling the loss of her death. So I nicknamed you Little Miss Missy in part because of the difficulty I was having and, in part, because it suited your very precocious personality."

Evie nodded understanding. "If it is too difficult for you…"

"Don't interrupt me. It's rude remember?" He said smiling raising a dark eyebrow.

Evie laughed. "Oh oui, of course! I apologize!"

"I will attempt to use your given name, per your request, when I remember to do so, if…" He paused. "…if you agree to continue to call my brother Père. We feel it important that your true paternity be kept a secret. Only the people in this room know the truth."

"But…? What about the man who was after me? That man with that horrible scar, that oily voice and those evil black eyes? Doesn't he know who I am?"

Vincent stepped forward then. "We don't think so Evie. Drakkar isn't one for details about the packages he is to deliver. And the man that sent him after you is dead. So, we believe the family's secret is safe."

"Oh…I see." She responded contemplatively. Then she looked at her father. "Honestly, I don't think I could have stopped calling Andre my Père. I have done so all my life." She smiled at Andre. "But, I will honor your wishes and keep a tight lid on our family's secret. Especially since it directly affects me personally." She grinned up at him.

"Bryce?" Vincent called him forward.

Bryce came forward and stood behind Evie slipping his arms around her waist.

"We..." Vincent motioned to everyone in the room. "We expect you to keep her safe."

"I won't let her out of my sight." Bryce promised him.

"Evie...Sasha should be whelping a new litter in about six weeks." Míchel said. "We have all discussed it and we think you should have another bodyguard."

"You want me to have two Míchel?" Evie exclaimed.

"Oui Mon Papillion." Bryce said softly, looking into her beautiful grey-green eyes. "*We* will need two, one for each of us."

"WE?" Evie narrowed her eyes. "What do you mean *WE*?"

"Hold the phone!" Alexis sprang to her feet. "Just wait one minute, Bryce Marten!"

Startled, Bryce turned to face his aunt. "Was it something I said?"

"It most certainly was!"

"Tante I..."

She closed the distance between them in a few short strides. Evie stepped aside so Alexis could stand directly in front of him.

In fact, the entire room took a few steps backward giving Alexis plenty of room.

"YOU! IT'S YOU! Alexis said poking him in the chest with her index finger.

"Me...? What Tante?" Bryce asked puzzled and just a little apprehensively.

Alexis narrowed her eyes at him. "You're Monsieur Papillion!"

"Oh merde!" Josie squeaked.

"Josephine!" Lucy admonished. "Language young lady!"

"Oops...sorry mama." She smiled.

Bryce shot her an accusing look.

"I didn't tell her! I swear!" Josie said defensively.

Alexis spun around to face her. "You knew? You knew and you didn't tell me?"

"He swore me to secrecy Tante. It's all *his* fault!" Josie deflected, pointing a finger at Bryce.

She turned to face Bryce once more. The room was so quiet you could hear a pin drop.

"Are you going to deny it?" She asked him accusingly.

"No Tante Lex. I am Monsieur Papillion." He said, resigned.

"Why didn't you tell me Cher? You are incredibly talented. Why didn't you want me to know?"

"Who the hell is Monsieur Papillion? Pierre broke the silence in the room.

Alexis began to point to several paintings throughout the room.

"*That* is Monsieur Papillion!" She said.

"You paint?" Rogét queried?

Andre blew out a long low whistle. "Wow, you are in a world of trouble! Lex, honey, don't kill him now..." He said laughing.

"Oh no. I have no intention of killing him. No, no, no. That would be far too easy."

"Now tante...let me explain." Bryce began.

"You!" She poked Bryce in the chest again.

Bryce shut his mouth.

"YOU promise me that you will put in an appearance at your showing next month!"

"But..."

"Promise me or there WILL be consequences!"

"But tante..."

"If you 'but Tante' me one more time Bryce Marten, I'll..." Alexis stepped closer to him poking his chest with her index finger.

"Okay! Okay! I'll make an appearance. Just don't hurt me." Bryce conceded throwing his hands up in surrender.

"Say it!" Alexis pushed.

Reluctantly, Bryce mumbled. "I promise."

"What?" Alexis put a cupped hand to her ear. "I can't hear you. What did you say?"

"Oh for the love of...!" He stopped short when he glanced around the room. All eyes were watching him silently pleading him to acquiesce. "Really? Fine! All right, I promise!"

Everyone in the room breathed a collective sigh of relief.

"Remind me to stay on your good side Mrs. DeGaul." Malcolm said from the corner of the room. "Andre I could use your wife when I need to interrogate a suspect! She's damn good!"

"Yes she is." Andre said, with pride and mischief in his voice.

Alexis smiled at Malcolm, and then scowled at her husband. "One more thing..." she said, looking at Evie.

"Anything for you Tante Lex..." Bryce said sweetly.

She looked back at him and smiled. "Take care of Evie. Promise me that you will do that too."

"Aw, now Tante... That, I can and will promise."

"Excuse me, but, does anyone in this room care about what *I* want?" Evie said in protest.

"NO!" Everyone in the room said in unison.

Then they all laughed.

"Just checking!" Evie said as she slipped back into Bryce's waiting arms. "Had to ask... you know...just in case anybody cared about *MY* opinion."

Rogét was seated in his chair in the situation room tapping on his keyboard. Now that the crisis was over, he could relax and maybe chat with his friend. She was sometimes very illusive which intrigued him. She was sweet and innocently naïve. She was also in trouble. Although his friend had never come right out and said so, he knew that there was more to her story than she revealed. He opened a chat window and found that she had already sent him a message. The first message read:

> Hello my sweet friend… I just wanted to send you a quick little note because I will be unavailable for the next day or two. My master is in town and I am obligated to be with him. I hope to chat with you soon ☺… ~Elise

He smiled to himself until he read the second message…

> Hello again my sweet friend… I only have a moment so I must be brief. My master is in a foul mood this evening and I have already been warned that our coming together will not be gentle. He placed a hand on my thigh during dinner and squeezed…hard. THAT is always an indication that there will be no tenderness… How I wish things were different for me… There is so much that I have yet to tell you. Someday my friend… someday. ~Elise

Roget felt anger and a sudden since of foreboding. He sat back in his chair and contemplated.

About the Author

Nienna Luinwe began her story telling as a young child with a vivid imagination and the gift of gab. She entertained herself and her sister with imaginative stories of action and adventure. She began writing down her short stories when she was a Senior in High School. Now she is very excited to introduce her very first novel. Feel free to visit her Facebook page or send her a message at Nienna.Luinwe@att.net.

Connect with Nienna Luinwe

Friend me on Facebook: https://www.facebook.com/nienna.luinwe.54
Favorite my Smashwords author page:
https://www.smashwords.com/profile/view/NiennaL